# The White Rider

Also available by Chris Priestley:

**DEATH AND THE ARROW**
*The first Tom Marlowe adventure*

# The White Rider

*A Tom Marlowe
Adventure*

## CHRIS PRIESTLEY

**DOUBLEDAY**

London • New York • Toronto • Sydney • Auckland

# For Helen

THE WHITE RIDER
A DOUBLEDAY BOOK 0 385 60694 X

Published in Great Britain by Doubleday,
an imprint of Random House Children's Books

This edition published 2004

1 3 5 7 9 10 8 6 4 2

Copyright © Chris Priestley, 2004

The right of Chris Priestley to be identified as the author of this work has
been asserted in accordance with the Copyright, Designs and Patents Act 1988.

Papers used by Random House Children's Books are natural, recyclable
products made from wood grown in sustainable forests. The manufacturing
processes conform to the environmental regulations of the country of origin.

Set in 13½/17½pt Bembo by
Falcon Oast Graphic Art Ltd.

RANDOM HOUSE CHILDREN'S BOOKS
61–63 Uxbridge Rd, London W5 5SA
A division of The Random House Group Ltd

RANDOM HOUSE AUSTRALIA (PTY) LTD
20 Alfred Street, Milsons Point, Sydney,
New South Wales 2061, Australia

RANDOM HOUSE NEW ZEALAND LTD
18 Poland Road, Glenfield, Auckland 10, New Zealand

RANDOM HOUSE (PTY) LTD
Endulini, 5A Jubilee Road, Parktown 2193, South Africa

THE RANDOM HOUSE GROUP Limited Reg. No. 954009
www.kidsatrandomhouse.co.uk

A CIP catalogue record for this book is available from the British Library.

Printed and bound in Great Britain
by Clays Ltd, St Ives plc

# Tower HILL

A chill breeze blew from east of the City, carrying on its breath the rancid taint of glue works and tanners' yards. It filled the sails of merchantmen and barges and shivered the surface of the Thames. It twisted the weather vanes on the turrets of the Tower of London and ruffled the black drapes on the scaffold on Tower Hill.

Grim-faced soldiers gripped their pikes and sword hilts while the crowd shifted their feet and blew on their hands to ward off the cold. There was a general muttering and grumbling about the wait, and the occasional chuckle and guffaw about the news that Lord Nithsdale had escaped from the Tower the day before dressed as a woman.

And in among the crowd was Tom Marlowe, fifteen years old – though he was soon to be sixteen – and the assistant of the man who stood at his side: the brilliant Dr Josiah Harker. Dr Harker had given no explanation why he wanted them to come to Tower Hill, but Tom had been through so much with the doctor in recent months that he would have followed him into a burning house without question.

A murmur ran through the onlookers as the Earl of Derwentwater finally mounted the scaffold. Tom wondered at how calm he looked, and his voice sounded clear when he turned to the crowd and spoke. After saying a few prayers, Derwentwater retracted his guilty plea and spoke warmly in praise of the exiled son of James II: James Francis Edward Stuart, the man he believed should rightfully be sitting on the throne now occupied by George I.

Tom listened as Derwentwater told the crowd that there would never be peace in the country until the Stuarts were restored to the throne, but few in England would have shared that view. They wanted no more papists on the throne.

The new King George may have been German, but he was a Protestant. Better a foreigner than a

# Tower Hill

Catholic. There would be no James III despite all the efforts of his supporters, the Jacobites.

'I die a Roman Catholic,' said Derwentwater. 'I am in perfect charity with all the world – I thank God for it – even with those of the present government, who are the most instrumental in my death.'

There were more murmurs, though Tom could not tell whether they were murmurs against Derwentwater or against the government.

'I freely forgive such ungenerously reported false things of me,' continued Derwentwater. 'And I hope to be forgiven the trespasses of my youth, by the Father of infinite mercy, into whose hands I commend my soul.'

He handed the paper on which his speech had been written to the sheriff and looked at the wooden block in front of him. Laughter rippled through the crowd as he asked the axeman to chip off a splinter of wood in case he hurt his neck. Then Derwentwater took off his coat and his waistcoat and kneeled down. A hush fell as he laid his head on the block.

'Lord Jesu receive my soul,' he prayed as the axe was raised. 'Lord Jesu receive my soul. Lord Jesu receive my soul—'

The axe fell and Tom shut his eyes and wished he could have shut his ears to the noise of the axe's striking. But when he opened his eyes there was even more horror and he turned away from the sight, but not before he had caught a glimpse of the axeman holding Derwentwater's head aloft for the crowd to see.

'Behold the head of a traitor!' he shouted. 'God save King George!'

The crowd erupted into cheering and booing, but again, Tom found it impossible to tell whether they were cheering Derwentwater or the king, or booing a traitor or the government that killed him.

The body was wrapped in black and taken away and then Lord Kenmure appeared. Tom thought how much harder it must be to come to the scaffold when it was already damp with blood. Kenmure had pleaded for mercy at his trial; but he stood bravely now, though he made no speech. He prayed, said a couple of words to the axeman and kneeled before the block.

This time Tom turned away and watched Dr Harker's face. He heard the axe come down once, then again. The doctor did not flinch either time, but looked straight ahead, even when the executioner once more said the words, 'Behold the head of a traitor,' and Tom knew what his friend must be seeing. Still he stared fixedly while the cheering and jeering broke out once more. His gaze did not waver, even when the crowd, encouraged by the soldiers, began to move away and disperse. Tom had to tug hard on the doctor's arm before his trance was broken, and when he turned to Tom he had tears in his eyes. He closed them and shook his head.

'I should not have brought you here, Tom,' he said. 'You should not have seen this. I am sorry, truly I am.'

'Why were you so determined that we came?' asked Tom.

'Well, Tom, I wanted—' began the doctor, but he was interrupted by a man standing behind him.

'Josiah Harker, as I live and breathe,' he said, clapping a hand on Dr Harker's shoulder.

'Who the devil . . . ? I don't believe it! Daniel . . . Well, how are you, man?'

The two men embraced like long-lost brothers, slapping each other's shoulders and laughing like schoolboys. It seemed a long time before Dr Harker remembered that Tom was with him.

'Daniel, Daniel,' he said, slightly out of breath. 'You must meet my very able assistant and good friend Thomas Marlowe. Tom, this is a very old friend of mine, Daniel Thornley.'

'I am delighted to make your acquaintance, Tom,' said Thornley, shaking Tom by the hand.

'And I yours,' said Tom.

Thornley was tall, and though he was probably a similar age to Dr Harker, he was leaner and fitter. He had a huge bright smile, his cheeks pulling back in curved creases to accommodate it. He had a relaxed air about him that put Tom immediately at ease, but his clothes were cheap and ill fitting, at odds with his voice and his bearing.

'What brings you here, Josiah?' asked Thornley, nodding his head towards the scaffold that was already being stripped of its black drapes.

'I might ask the same thing,' said Dr Harker.

'I have a professional interest in these matters, as you know, Josiah.'

'Yes, of course.' Dr Harker's smile faded a little. 'I suppose I had hoped you might have changed trades.'

Thornley smiled and then narrowed his eyes as he seemed to catch sight of something over Tom's shoulder. Tom followed his gaze but saw nothing but the remnants of the dispersing crowd.

'Let us not rekindle this old debate, Josiah,' said Thornley. 'I must go now, in any case. Shall we meet again? Do you still frequent The Quill coffee house?'

'Yes, I do,' said Dr Harker. 'But how do you know—?'

'Splendid, splendid. Then I shall see you in there very soon, Josiah. Very nice to meet you, Tom.'

Thornley walked off into the crowd and, with what seemed to Tom an almost supernatural ease, disappeared into it.

# 2

## Monsieur PETIT

A golden haze lay across London like a silk scarf, softening the shapes of buildings, muting the colours. It conjured up something beautiful and dreamlike out of the cold, damp morning. Even the usual forge-like clatter and clang of the city seemed to have stilled itself in sympathy with the scene.

Frost silvered the grass of St Bride's churchyard, twinkling as it began to melt, and made the shadows in the carvings on the gravestones shimmer blue. Cobwebs glistened, strung with pearl-like beads of water. The wrought-iron gate creaked at Tom's touch.

He left the slippery flagstone path leading to the church, walked across the wet grass and stopped in front of a headstone. The stone looked fresh save for a light coating of London grime; a year had not much weathered it and the carving was still as sharp as the day it was chiselled. A blackbird landed on a nearby railing, its tail rising as it rocked first forwards then back. It opened its yellow beak and sang out loud and long, its throat quivering, its wings twitching. Then it flew off, chattering away into the distance. Silence returned.

HERE LIES THE BODY OF WILL PIGGOT. Tom still found it hard to read the words, and even in the reading of them he found it harder still to accept that his friend really did lie beneath his feet and that he would never again see his face or hear his voice. It was hard to bear and Tom closed his eyes and hung his head.

'Here I am, Will,' said Tom without looking up. 'Here to show I haven't forgotten you. Nor ever will.' He opened his eyes and looked at the headstone once more.

On these visits to Will's grave, Tom increasingly found himself talking to the slightly startled-looking cherub that was carved into the top of the headstone above a scroll with REST IN PEACE written across it. It made him smile. Will could not have been farther from a cherub in life, and yet . . . and yet, there was something of Will in that carved cherub: the crooked smile, the long jaw and the deer-like alertness that had served him so well. Until the day of his murder, that is.

Will's friendship and, more especially, his untimely death, had changed Tom Marlowe's life for ever. Though Tom would have given anything to have Will standing there with him again, the tragedy had set Tom on an adventure that had made his life a thousand times richer than before. It was something that made him feel more than a little guilty: that he should have gained in any way from poor Will's terrible death.

If Will had not been murdered he would probably still be apprenticed to his father at the Lamb and Lion printing house, and he would certainly never have met the amazing Ocean Carter. Will had been Ocean's friend too, and Ocean had joined forces with Tom and Dr Harker to track down his killer. He was like no one Tom had ever met before; a cat-like visitor from London's underworld, quick-witted and fearless.

And now Ocean worked for Tom's father in his place and Tom worked for Dr Harker, cataloguing the doctor's enormous collection of artefacts collected on his travels and adventures around the world, living in an attic room at the top of his house in Fleet Street.

'You used to love to hear about Dr Harker's travels, didn't you, Will?' said Tom. 'You'd have loved to see all the things we've been cataloguing. We used to talk about how we'd run away to sea one day, didn't we? We used to say we'd go to America and seek our fortunes. I wonder if we ever would have done?'

Tom sat down on the cold stone tomb nearby, looked at the cherub smiling back at him and closed his eyes against the tears.

'Morning, Tom,' said Ocean as Tom walked into the printing house. He wiped as much ink from his hand as he could and offered it to Tom, who shook it warmly, slapping him on the arm.

'How are you, Ocean?' Tom asked. 'Father still keeping you busy?'

'I should say so, Tom,' he replied. 'It's all right for you, sitting around all day looking at books and the like. Some of us have real work to do.'

'I've done my share of work in this place,' said Tom, patting one of the presses warmly. 'I miss it sometimes, though. Is he about? Dr Harker's fussing about his books.'

'He's in the shop, Tom,' said Ocean. 'He'll be glad to see you.'

Tom walked through the door and found Mr Marlowe sitting deep in concentration, surrounded by piles of prints.

'Tom!' Mr Marlowe looked up from a print he was

reading. 'Just reading this sermon about how we are all about to be consumed by hell fire. "The Day of Judgement is upon us . . . These are the Last Days." I can't think how many of these I've printed in my life; yet here we all are.' He chuckled to himself as he got up and clapped his huge hands on Tom's shoulders. 'It's good to see you, son.'

'And you, Father,' said Tom. 'Dr Harker wondered if his books were back from the binders yet.'

'Not yet, no. Tell him they'll be done by Friday.'

'I will, Father,' said Tom, dropping his voice to a conspiratorial whisper. 'How's Ocean getting on?'

'He's a godsend, to be honest, Tom,' said Mr Marlowe. 'You'd think he'd been in the business all his life. He's a deep one, though. A bit like you in that respect.'

Tom returned Mr Marlowe's smile. 'I do believe you're growing fond of Ocean, Father.'

'I am,' said Mr Marlowe, as if the thought had only that instant entered his head. 'I believe I am.' He blushed slightly at the realization that not so long ago he would never have countenanced even employing a man of Ocean's shady background. He had disapproved of Tom's friendship with Will Piggot, and taking Ocean on had been a kind of penance after Will's murder. But now he found that he simply liked having Ocean around, and it helped sweeten the loss of Tom to Dr Harker. 'And by the way,' he went on.

'What's this I hear about Dr Harker taking you to Tower Hill, Tom?'

'To the execution, yes,' said Tom. 'It was horrible, Father.'

'I can't say that I approve, Tom,' said Mr Marlowe. 'I don't have any great sympathy for those Jacobite traitors, but even so . . . It's a grim piece of entertainment for a lad of your age. Why did Harker feel the need to go?'

'I'm not altogether sure,' Tom replied. 'He said we would be witnessing history, but I'm not sure there wasn't more to it than that.'

'These Jacobite rascals are everywhere, Tom. Mr Finch was in yesterday – you know, the baker on Goat Lane whose brother is a turnkey in Newgate? He says that London is crawling with them. He says that people think they're all Scottish, but they have scores of sympathizers in England . . . and in this very city. Think of that, Tom: in this very city. He says you can't tell who they might be, neither. It might be someone you've known for years. They'll get more than they bargained for if they come here, I'll tell you that for nothing.' Mr Marlowe picked up a hammer and weighed it in his hand. 'You can't trust anyone, that's what Finch says. You can't trust anyone. That's what the world's come to, Tom. It's all good for business though, I have to say. The printing house has never been busier, with all the pamphlets and sermons being churned out.'

'You don't think that . . .' began Tom and then shook his head.

'What is it, Tom?'

'You don't think it possible that Dr Harker might be a Jacobite sympathizer, do you?'

'Dr Harker!' said Mr Marlowe with a laugh. 'Never!' But then he saw the serious look on Tom's face and furrowed his brow. 'Why would you think such a thing?'

'It's just that . . . it's just a feeling I have about the execution. There was something more to it than Dr Harker was saying.'

'Come on, Tom,' said Mr Marlowe. 'After all you've been through with Dr Harker, you can't believe he would lie to you? He doesn't seem the type for secrets. He probably just thought seeing an execution would be educational. You can't get everything out of books.'

When Tom turned the corner into the courtyard of Dr Harker's house, he took out his watch and remembered that the doctor had said that he had some business and would be out until ten o'clock. However, the maid, Sarah, would let him in and Tom was more than happy to while away the time in Dr Harker's study.

To his surprise, though, when Sarah opened the

door she said she was sure the doctor was in because she had heard him walking about as she cleaned. So Tom climbed the stairs to the study. Above him, he heard raised voices: one was Dr Harker's, but the other he did not recognize. He was about to lay his hand on the brass doorknob of the study, when he paused.

The door was very slightly ajar and Tom could just see Dr Harker. He was talking to another man who was seated with his back to Tom. As Tom peered into the room, the man handed something to the doctor. Tom could not see what it was, save that it glinted as it caught the light from the nearby window. Dr Harker studied it and then put it in his waistcoat pocket. Tom knocked at the door and walked in. The stranger jumped up and reached into his pocket. Dr Harker grabbed his arm.

'Tom!' said the doctor with a rather forced laugh. 'Come in, come in. I would like you to meet my friend, Monsieur . . . Petit.'

The two men exchanged a furtive glance and then the stranger smiled and held out a hand. '*Bonjour,* Tom,' he said, with a thick French accent. 'I am very pleased to meet you.'

The man was tall and broad shouldered. Although the clothes he wore were stylish – verging on the foppish even – and obviously expensive, his appearance was a little dishevelled. As he took Tom's hand Tom noticed that his lace cuff was frayed and grubby.

# Monsieur PETIT

He seemed an unlikely friend for Dr Harker.

Monsieur Petit's broad and handsome face was unshaven, the bristles, like his eyebrows, fair, and though his smile was warm enough, his clear grey eyes studied Tom with a wolf-like intensity. Tom was forced to look away and turned to Dr Harker.

'Monsieur . . . Petit is in London for a few days on business,' said the doctor, once again exchanging a glance with his guest that Tom felt he was not supposed to see. 'He is in the silk trade, with family in Spitalfields.' Tom thought that a man in the silk trade ought to have cleaner cuffs. 'He was just leaving.'

The stranger bowed and shook Dr Harker's hand and they spoke earnestly to each other in French for a couple of minutes, Tom's frustration at not being able to understand them growing by the second.

'*Au revoir*,' said Monsieur Petit, turning to Tom. '*Au revoir*, Josiah.'

'I'll see you out,' said Dr Harker, and the two men left and descended the stairs.

Tom crept to the stairwell and peered down. At the bottom, instead of making for the front door, they turned towards the back of the house. Tom went to the window to see the stranger leaving by the back courtyard. As he lifted the latch of the door in the courtyard wall, the stranger turned and looked up. Tom leaped sideways out of view. Had he been seen?

He was not sure.

Tom could hear Dr Harker's footsteps as he began to climb the stairs and he retreated back into the study. When the doctor entered, Tom was doing a very good job of looking fascinated by a book of geometry.

'Sorry about that, Tom,' said Dr Harker, taking off his wig and scratching at his scalp. 'Ah – that's better. Haven't seen Petit there for years.'

'Really?' said Tom, trying to sound uninterested. 'Have you known him for long, then?'

'Oh yes. For many years.'

'How do you know him?' Tom asked.

'How?' said Dr Harker, looking a little flustered. 'I don't know, Tom. I . . . erm . . . You know how it is, Tom.'

Tom had no idea how it was, but said nothing.

'But enough of Monsieur Petit!' The doctor slapped his hand down on a pile of books. 'It is your birthday tomorrow, is it not? Your sixteenth birthday?'

'Well, yes it is, Dr Harker,' said Tom.

'Then we must mark it in some way, don't you think? Of course we must! What do you say, Tom? What shall we do?'

'Well, sir, I should love to go to the theatre. My father never wanted to go and—'

'Excellent!' said Dr Harker. 'The theatre it shall be! We'll have a marvellous time.'

'Thank you, Dr Harker,' said Tom. 'But what shall

we see?'

'Well, I really think that ought to be for you to decide. What will it be, Tom? Shakespeare? Johnson?'

'I rather thought that I might like to see . . .' began Tom.

'Yes?' said Dr Harker with a smile.

'Well, I rather thought I might like to see an opera, Dr Harker.'

The doctor's face fell. 'An opera, you say?'

'Yes,' said Tom. 'But if you would rather . . .'

'No, no,' said Dr Harker, regaining his good cheer. 'If you want to see an opera, then an opera you shall see.'

Tom grinned.

'Excellent,' the doctor added, a little hesitantly. 'Excellent . . .'

Tom and Dr Harker were soon hard at work on the doctor's collection. Shelf by shelf, drawer by drawer, item after item would be taken out and dusted down and given a label with its own number. Tom would ask Dr Harker what the item was called and would then make an entry in his best script in a huge leather-bound ledger on the doctor's desk.

Of course, this process was not a swift one, as every time Tom asked what an item was, it would trigger a lecture about its history and the people who made it and a lengthy reminiscence about the adventure connected with collecting it. Neither Tom nor the doctor in any way minded this, though; for Tom it was an education and for Dr Harker it was a chance to relive the excitement of his youth and give vent to his enthusiasm for his treasures.

Tom dreamed of travelling, and Dr Harker's tales of his own travels fed his dreams. Normally, Tom would listen intently to every word the doctor said, sailing away with him in his imagination, paddling canoes along twisting rivers, riding horses across wide open plains, but today he found himself letting the words drift away into the background while the voice of the stranger he had met earlier grew in volume.

For Monsieur Petit might have been speaking French when he left, but he was speaking English when Tom arrived at the study door, he was sure of that. And more – much more strange than that, he had been speaking with a very particular accent: a *Scottish* accent.

## 3

# Temple BAR

Italian opera was all the rage and Tom was eager to see what all the fuss was about. Dr Harker, however, was not at all keen on this new craze. To him the London stage seemed full of pantomimes and harlequinades and a lot of trilling Italians singing utter nonsense, but he kept his views to himself for once, as he and Tom braved the evening crowds and headed west for the King's Theatre in Haymarket. Mr Marlowe hated all kinds of theatre and, as Tom had expected, had politely turned the offer down.

As they walked along the Strand, a newspaper seller sucked in a wheezy breath and yelled for all he was worth in a thin, rasping voice: 'The White Rider strikes again! Ghostly highwayman robs another coach!'

Dr Harker's interest was aroused immediately. He bought a paper and pointed to the story. 'Do you see this, Tom?' he said. 'I've been following this story for the last few weeks. Do you see? The White Rider is a highwayman ... but not just *any* highwayman. Witnesses say that he is a kind of spectre or phantom, with a skull for a face—'

'A skull?' asked Tom.

'Yes,' said Dr Harker with a smile. 'Imagine that! It's intriguing, is it not? And there is more. He is said to be able to kill simply by pointing at his victims. Now what do you make of that?'

'I ... I ... don't know,' said Tom. 'Maybe the witnesses are mistaken.'

'Maybe. But this is the sixth such incident, all in different locations with different witnesses. They all seem to have seen the same thing.'

'Maybe the newspapers have made the whole thing up,' Tom suggested. 'Father said they do that all the time.'

Dr Harker laughed. 'Mr Marlowe may well be right,' he said. 'He often is. This White Rider has been striking around London. Perhaps we shall find out for ourselves whether he is a phantom or not.'

Tom was not quite as keen on this idea as Dr Harker seemed to be. Besides, he had been trying to work up the courage and find the right time to ask Dr Harker a rather delicate question.

'Dr Harker,' he said, 'can I ask you something?'

'Of course, Tom. Anything, you know that.'

'Is Monsieur Petit a Jacobite?'

Tom had not known how Dr Harker would react, but he had certainly not expected him to grab him by the collar and nearly pull him off his feet.

The doctor bundled Tom into a nearby alleyway. He looked about him and his manner was so excited that Tom was actually frightened of him.

'Listen to me, Tom,' he whispered. 'There is deadly danger in that question. Deadly danger, Tom. Do you understand?'

'Yes,' said Tom, though he understood nothing save Dr Harker's utter seriousness.

The doctor edged him to the corner of the street and pointed back the way they had come, towards Temple Bar and Fleet Street. 'Do you see, Tom?' he asked. 'Up on Temple Bar?'

Tom followed Dr Harker's pointing finger. On metal spikes above the arch of Temple Bar, silhouetted against the evening sky, were the boiled and tarred heads of Derwentwater and Kenmure.

'Do you want my head up there, Tom?' said Dr Harker.

'No, sir,' said Tom. 'Of course I don't.'

'Then, understand that we must never speak of Monsieur Petit again.' The words sounded like a threat.

'I understand,' said Tom.

Dr Harker suddenly saw the fear in Tom's eyes and allowed his face to relax into a smile. 'If I keep things from you, it is to keep you safe, Tom.'

Tom nodded and Dr Harker brushed Tom's coat down, adjusted his lace cuffs and tapped his cane loudly on the pavement. 'Good,' he said, regaining his previous relaxed manner. 'Good. Then let us away to the theatre.'

Tom had been so frozen by Dr Harker's words and fierce attitude that everything else in the surrounding world seemed to freeze along with him. In the alley there had seemed to be no sound other than that of Dr Harker's intense whispering voice, but as they emerged again, the rich cacophony of London life rolled back in like a mighty wave and crashed over them.

Carriages rumbled over the cobbles, shoppers milled about, staring in windows and chattering. Tom recovered his good spirits as they walked past Charing Cross, and the deadly danger Dr Harker spoke of seemed already a world away as they turned into the Haymarket. Tom was determined to enjoy himself.

Dr Harker had the use of a box that was reserved

by a friend of his from the Royal Society, so they could avoid the scrum of people as they tried to find their seats. Once in their box overlooking the stage, they could look down on the rowdy benches below and the crowded galleries behind them.

An orchestra was playing but it could not be heard above the noise of young rakes yelling drunkenly at each other, friends hailing each other from yards away and a general thunderous rumble as the audience chattered and gossiped. A group of men in the gallery began singing – a bawdy song unconnected with the music the orchestra was doggedly playing.

A hat was taken from an old man's head and flung across the theatre, to loud cheering from the gallery. A half-eaten orange flew past and hit a young lady on the side of the face, prompting her beau to get to his feet with his hand on his sword hilt, but as he had no idea where the fruit had come from he was forced to sit down again, to loud, derisive laughter.

The opera was called *Harlequin in Love*, and Tom wondered how it was going to compete with the drama the audience had created before the perform-ance, but he need not have worried. Though Dr Harker shook his head in dismay, Tom was spell-bound, as the singers appeared in ever more elaborate costumes in front of extravagantly painted backdrops. Cymbals crashed, small explosions flashed and banged, and a flock of small birds were released and flew in panic around the theatre, settling on wigs and spattering hats with their droppings.

Tom had not the faintest idea what was going on, of course, as the words, even if he could have made them out, were sung in Italian, but the spectacle of it enthralled him. He was particularly taken with the actress dressed as a man who sang a particularly sad song towards the end of the opera.

'Did you enjoy that?' asked Dr Harker when they were outside afterwards.

'Yes,' said Tom. 'Immensely. Though I could see that you were not impressed.'

'No, no,' began the doctor with a sigh. 'Well . . . Actually, Tom, the truth is, I hated it.'

Tom laughed and Dr Harker joined him.

'I'm sorry, sir,' said Tom. 'I hope it was not too much of a trial for you.'

'I think I will recover soon enough,' said Dr Harker with a smile. 'But I must say I could do with some air. The night is still young, Tom. What say we take a stroll by the river?'

'I'd like that, sir,' said Tom, who was hoping he would be brave enough to broach the subject of the mysterious Monsieur Petit again.

'So what was it you most enjoyed?' asked Dr Harker as they walked besides the Thames.

'Oh, the actress who sang the song near the end.'

'The astonishingly plump one?' asked Dr Harker in a baffled voice.

'No, sir,' said Tom, surprised that there could be any confusion. 'Not her. The one who was dressed as a man.'

'The one who . . . was . . . dressed . . .' the doctor began. He stopped and looked at Tom with raised eyebrows. 'The one who was dressed as a man!' he repeated, and to Tom's surprise he collapsed into roaring laughter and had to support himself on his cane.

'Dr Harker?' said Tom, a little annoyed now. 'What is it that is so funny?'

The doctor pulled himself upright and, taking a silk handkerchief from his pocket, dabbed at the tears in his eyes. 'Oh dear, oh my word,' he said, taking deep breaths to control himself. 'That was no actress, young Marlowe. That was a castrato.'

Tom could see it was taking an effort of will for the doctor to stop himself laughing again. 'A cast— cast— A what, sir?' he said in exasperation.

'A castrato, Tom.'

'So she was a castrato? And what is that, if I may ask?'

'It's *he*,' said Dr Harker with a sigh and a grin. 'A castrato is . . . Well . . . a castrato is . . . How can I put this . . . ?'

Dr Harker's words petered out and he squinted

over Tom's shoulder into the distance. Tom turned and saw that there was a small commotion some way off ahead of them. A group of boatmen and passers-by were clustered around some steps leading down to the river and the ferry boats moored there. Dr Harker walked purposefully towards them and Tom followed.

As they got nearer they could hear that the voices of the boatmen, usually so raucous and curse-laden, were strangely hushed. Two of them held lanterns over their heads and the light from them swayed back and forth, making the shadows flex and stretch, as if the quay itself were afloat on a choppy sea. As Tom and Dr Harker reached the top of the slimy steps, they could see that one of the boatmen had a punting pole and was prodding about between the ferry boats with great concentration.

'He's gone under again . . . No, no, there he is . . . If I can just get the pole under him and . . .'

The water was as black as strong coffee. Suddenly something bobbed to the surface between the ferry hulls. Tom could not make out what it was at first. It was covered in lank brown hair. A dead dog perhaps? Another prod by the ferry men left no doubt, as the thing spun round in the water. It was a human head, and the rest of the body rose up to the surface with a sickening whoosh, its clothes billowing around in the inky waters.

# 4

# The SKEAN-DHU

Tom shuddered and let out an involuntary groan as the body bobbed up and down in the black water, its bloodless face as white as the lace at its throat.

An old man standing nearby turned and grinned gap-toothed from under his crumpled, broad-brimmed hat. 'Another what's had a bit too much of the Geneva,' he said and cackled. 'Eh? Eh? I said, another what's had too much of the gin.'

Tom did not answer and the old man cackled

again. The ferrymen heaved the body up onto the quayside and it slapped down wetly onto the stonework like a pile of newly washed clothes.

Just as they did so Under-marshal Hitchin appeared, silver baton in hand, with his motley guard of thugs and ruffians. Tom and Dr Harker had had previous dealings with the odious Hitchin, and he in turn remained deeply suspicious of them both. He smiled wolfishly at Tom as he passed by, and Tom moved a little closer to Dr Harker.

The under-marshal shoved the old man aside and made his way forward. 'Make way, make way,' he said. 'Let me through, let me through. What have we got then? Another drunk gone swimming?'

'That's what I said, ain't it?' said the old man, turning to Tom with a self-satisfied smirk. 'Too much of the gin!'

'Anyone gone through his pockets?' said Hitchin, ignoring him.

The ferrymen shook their heads despite the fact that Tom had seen two of them doing just that only seconds before Hitchin arrived.

'Anybody know him?' No one answered. 'Well, then,' said Hitchin, turning to one of his men and waving in the direction of the body. 'Fetch a cart. The surgeons can play with him. And make sure you get paid this time!'

'Wait,' said Dr Harker.

Hitchin looked up. 'I do not much like being interrupted in my business, Doctor,' he said coldly. 'What is it?'

'And I apologize, of course. But I do not think he drowned,' said Dr Harker. 'Or at any rate, he did not *just* drown. I believe he was a Jacobite and I believe he was murdered.'

Hitchin paused for a minute and then laughed loudly, joined a moment later by his men. 'That's very good, Doctor.' He had stopped laughing now and looked coldly once more at Dr Harker. 'Now where's that cart?'

'Look at his arm,' said Dr Harker. 'His right forearm.'

'What has any of this got to do with you, may I ask?' Hitchin took a step towards Dr Harker.

'I am a citizen of London,' said the doctor. 'And you are in its employ. I need no other qualification. Now I ask you again, will you look at his arm – or do I have to send for a Justice of the Peace?'

Hitchin squinted at him and then reluctantly dropped onto his haunches to inspect the arm, grabbing a ferryman's light. Tom could see clearly now what the doctor had already spotted. There was a word, or at least some letters, tattooed on the arm: JAFRED. But what did it mean? The puzzled look on Hitchin's face asked the same question.

'It is a composite word,' Dr Harker explained. 'I've

seen it before. It is made up of the first two letters of his leader's forenames: James Francis Edward. He is a follower of James Stuart, the Pretender; a Jacobite agent.'

A murmur went round the group of ferrymen.

'Even if this was true,' said Hitchin with a bored sigh, 'what makes you so sure he was murdered?'

'Turn him over,' said Dr Harker.

'Do it,' ordered Hitchin.

Two of them rolled the body onto its front with another sickly wet-fish slap. Sticking out of its back, next to the shoulder blade, was the hilt of a small dagger. It seemed to Tom that everyone present turned to look at Dr Harker in amazement.

'I happened to see it as the body rolled over in the water,' said Dr Harker.

Hitchin pulled the dagger out and inspected it. The lantern light flickered across the wet blade. 'You mean to tell me that this little darning needle killed him?'

'It's possible,' said Dr Harker. 'But I think the fatal blow was probably struck with something larger.'

Sure enough, one of Hitchin's men found a tear in the man's coat that was probably a sword cut.

'Then why the dagger?' Hitchin asked.

'It is a skean-dhu,' said Dr Harker. Hitchin squinted in bafflement. 'A Scottish dagger,' the doctor continued. 'Someone wanted it to be known that this was a Jacobite rebel. They wish his colleagues to know he has been killed.'

'You seem to know a great deal about these Jacobites, Dr Harker,' said Hitchin suspiciously.

'I know a great deal about a great many things. I make no apology for it.'

'But one might wonder where your true sympathies lie,' said Hitchin. 'These are troubled times, are they not? Knowing about Jacobites is one thing but—'

'I know a great deal about fish,' interrupted Dr Harker. 'Does that make me a trout?'

One of Hitchin's men laughed for a few noisy seconds until a glance from the under-marshal silenced him.

'Don't think to bandy words with—' he began, but he was interrupted by the noisy arrival of a carriage and a group of armed men on horseback. They dismounted and ran down towards the steps, their boots clattering across the pavement. Two of them grabbed the body; the rest pointed cocked pistols at Hitchin's men.

'What's the meaning of this?' shouted Hitchin. 'Do you know who I am?'

Another knot of black-clad men came forward, holding pistols up to their chests. Several others took up positions around the carriage, watching the nearby building, pistols cocked. One of the men approached Hitchin and, without even looking at him, held out a letter.

He snatched it, read it, squinted at the messenger and handed the letter back. 'What do I say if someone comes for the body?' he asked as the man walked away again.

'What body?' came the reply as four of the men carried the body to a waiting carriage and threw it in. With a couple of shouts from the driver and a clatter of hooves the carriage and horsemen were gone, leaving Tom, Dr Harker, Hitchin and the others standing rather foolishly around the puddle that was the only tangible sign that the body had ever been there.

'Who was that, Hitchin?' said Dr Harker.

'That's Under-marshal Hitchin to you!' snapped Hitchin. 'And don't nobody forget it!' Then quietly, almost to himself, he said, 'I don't know. Government men.'

'But what about the murdered man?'

'Who cares?' said Hitchin. 'He was a Jacobite, like you said. It's just one of the vermin we won't have to hang.'

He gathered his men together and they began to move off, shoving bystanders out of the way in a transparent effort to regain some credibility in the face of such a public humiliation. But just as he was leaving, one of the ferrymen pointed up at the sky to the north-west over Tyburn and Hampstead beyond and shouted, 'Look at that!'

'Lord save us!' said another.

# The Skean-Dhu

Everyone, including Tom and Dr Harker, turned to follow the ferrymen's gaze, and there in the sky was a weird floating pale light with rainbow colours at its edge, flickering and drifting in and out of visibility.

'Extraordinary!' said Dr Harker. 'Look at this, Tom!'

'What is it, sir?' said Tom.

'I have no idea. Some freakish effect of nature. Some sort of optical marvel. Isn't it wonderful?'

'Come on,' said Hitchin to his men, sounding nervous and eager for this troubled night to end. 'Let's get out of here!'

'Extraordinary,' said Dr Harker, shaking his head and smiling up at the sky in wonderment. 'Quite extraordinary.'

## 5

# Death ON A PALE HORSE

A few days later, Tom and Dr Harker were walking through Ludgate on their way to The Quill coffee house. Tom had been over and over in his mind the events of recent days. During his many sleepless nights, his mind raced with images of axes and daggers, severed heads and floating bodies. People were now calling the strange lights in the sky Tom had seen that night 'The Earl of Derwentwater Lights' after the executed Jacobite lord.

It seemed to Tom that the whole Jacobite business

was pressing in around him, and he had failed to come to any conclusion about Dr Harker's involvement. He did not want to believe that the doctor was mixed up in the Jacobite cause, but the more he thought about it, the more there seemed to be no other sensible explanation. Tom had resolved to watch and wait.

Dr Harker seemed to sense Tom's troubled mind and put a hand on his shoulder as they walked. 'This is a great country, Tom,' he said, 'but it is also full of terrible darkness. Remember always that I care a great deal for your safety and would not see you harmed for all the world.'

Tom smiled and nodded. Dr Harker opened the door to The Quill and waved Tom inside with a theatrical flourish. 'After you, sir,' he said with a bow of his head.

Tom smiled weakly and went in, spoiling the effect slightly by tripping on the step and almost falling into the coffee house. Dr Harker scowled, but not at Tom's clumsiness. Someone was sitting in the doctor's favourite seat, his face hidden behind the newspaper he was reading. They were just looking for other seats when the newspaper dropped and Tom recognized Dr Harker's friend Thornley from Tower Hill.

'Dr Harker,' said Tom. 'It's Mr Thornley.'

'Josiah,' said Thornley, getting to his feet.

'Daniel.' Dr Harker smiled and shook the hand

he was offered. 'You have met Tom Marlowe here.'

'Pleased to meet you again, Master Marlowe,' said Thornley, shaking Tom's hand in turn.

'And I you, sir,' Tom replied.

'Splendid, splendid,' said Thornley.

Tom noticed that Thornley was quite changed since he last saw him. He was clean-shaven now and wore expensive clothes. Even so, they were black and sober and in no way flamboyant. Tom gained the swift impression that Thornley seemed almost to dress for the occasion in order to seem as inconspicuous as possible. It was certainly impossible to tell what trade he was in, let alone why it was that Dr Harker had hoped he might have changed it.

'Come – let's all sit down,' said Thornley. 'I can see why you come here, Josiah. The coffee is excellent.'

Dr Harker and Tom sat down and Thornley ordered drinks for them all, again remarking on the pleasant surprise of seeing them again so soon.

'Why are you here, Daniel?' said Dr Harker with an expressionless face.

'Same old Josiah' – Thornley smiled – 'always to the point.'

'Why are you here?' repeated Dr Harker. 'What do you want? It is wonderful to see you, of course, and I hope we shall have a chance to talk about old times and dine together, but please – why have you come? It certainly is not to tell me that the coffee here is excellent. Though it is.'

The smile disappeared momentarily from Thornley's face. 'These are dangerous times, Josiah,' he said. 'I wonder if you realize how dangerous?'

'I was saying something similar to our young friend here, not ten minutes ago,' Dr Harker replied.

'And yet I hear you were openly speaking Scotch the other night. Do you think that wise?'

'I was not speaking "Scotch", as you put it, Daniel. I merely gave the correct name for the dagger the poor unfortunate man was stabbed with. Is that a crime now, in this great country of ours?'

'Yes!' snapped Thornley, thumping his hand down on the table. Customers nearby turned and frowned at them. There was a tense pause before Thornley calmed himself and dropped his voice once more. 'Listen to me, Josiah. You are a very clever man, but you need to show more common sense. Have you had any visitors?'

Tom looked at his friend and thought of the strange Monsieur Petit.

'No,' said Dr Harker. 'I have had no visitors.'

Thornley looked hard at him and then at Tom, but Tom said nothing. Just then a huge commotion erupted at a nearby table.

'It's a disgrace!'

'Hang the lot of them!'

'It's not safe to leave the city!'

'It's not safe *in* the city either!'

'If they spent as much time chasing highwaymen as they do chasing Jacobites the country might be a better place for honest folk. What say you, Dr Harker?' The speaker was a stout, red-faced man at the next table.

'If they spent a little more time mending the roads, life would certainly be better for honest backsides,' said Dr Harker, to some laughter. 'But I see you are not in a joking mood today. What has especially upset you?'

'My brother here has been the victim of highway robbery,' said his friend.

'Then he should be grateful,' said Thornley, settling back into his chair.

'Grateful? How so?'

'For escaping with his life,' replied Thornley with a broad smile that was not returned.

'You must forgive my friend,' said Dr Harker, giving Thornley a weary look. 'He means no harm. He enjoys playing the cynic. But there is something in what he says, after all. Whatever was stolen, at least your brother is safe and well. That at least is cause for some cheer.'

'Yes, Dr Harker,' said the brother, still looking suspiciously at Thornley. 'I am of course grateful that I was not harmed. But another fellow traveller was not so lucky.'

Dr Harker shook his head. 'What is this about your fellow passenger?'

'Murdered, he was,' said the man. 'Murdered in cold blood.' As he spoke, he suddenly looked a little self-conscious: the whole coffee house was now looking at him and hanging on his every word. Everyone, that is, Tom noticed, except Thornley, who had half closed his eyes as if the whole subject bored him.

'Go on, sir,' urged Dr Harker.

'Well,' said the man, 'I had some business to attend to in Oxford – I am a clockmaker by trade – and was returning to London by stagecoach. We had not travelled long before I fell into conversation with my fellow passengers: an innkeeper from Southwark, a haberdasher from Cheapside and a tobacco grower from the Americas. The innkeeper was an enthusiastic talker, entertaining us with a great many colourful stories. It seemed a long time before anyone else had a chance to speak.

'The fellow from the Americas, when he did speak, was equally entertaining. The Americas were far more dangerous than England for the traveller, with not only bandits to fear, but bloodthirsty savages to boot. He said he always carried a pistol just in case and was an excellent shot. I confess I found it a comfort to have him aboard, as I for one had no experience of bandits and had no wish to gain any.

'He had many fascinating tales of the Colonies and

made the journey fly by. His charm was only increased by the knowledge that he bravely carried some deformity in his right hand. Though he wore a glove to conceal it, it was evident the hand was ruined in some way. Yet here was a man who was brimming with confidence and self-reliance. He was an inspiration, sir . . . and yet we were to see him shot down like an animal.' The clockmaker looked down and wiped his brow, the tips of his fingers disappearing under his wig as he did so.

'A brandy for my friend here,' said Dr Harker.

'No,' said the clockmaker, raising his hand. 'Thank you, but no. I do not drink intoxicating spirits. I am well, thank you. But I am not used to such scenes. It has disturbed me a great deal.'

'It is perfectly natural,' said Dr Harker. 'I should not have pressed you to report the matter. Forgive me.'

'No, I will speak. If only to tell you of the extraordinary nature of our attacker.'

'Extraordinary? Extraordinary in what way?'

'Well' – the clockmaker took a breath and seemed to search for the words – 'the man – if man he was – had no face . . . or no face to speak of. Where a face should have been there was only the white bones of a skull. Even as I say the words I doubt the powers of my own senses, but I swear to you that I saw what I say I saw.'

'The White Rider!' exclaimed Dr Harker. 'I knew

it!' There was a murmur of recognition. The doctor was clearly not the only customer of The Quill to have been following the story.

'You know of this creature?'

'Only by reputation,' Dr Harker replied. 'Come, tell us everything, my friend. Omit nothing. You were talking to another passenger. Then what happened?'

'Well, sir, the first inkling we had that anything was amiss was when we heard a loud bang, which I now take to have been a pistol shot, and the coach skidded to a halt. Then a voice outside shouted for us to stay where we were if we wanted to live. I leaned out of the window, looked in the direction of the voice and that was when I saw—'

'You saw a highwayman,' suggested Dr Harker. 'The skull-faced highwayman? The White Rider?'

'Yes. He was sitting on a white horse, and a strange glow was emanating from the ground in front of him and from the smoke billowing about him, so that he looked more like a creature from hell than of this world. Then he rode towards us. It was a fearful sight.'

'Did this apparition speak?' asked Dr Harker.

'Yes, it did,' said the clockmaker. 'In a loud voice, he shouted, "Gentlemen! Do as I say and none will be harmed, but be sure that I will punish any mis-behaviour most speedily. I only want your valuables, but I will take your life if needs be." Then suddenly the man from the Americas shouted, "This is outrageous! We will not give in to such knavery!"' and made for the door. I struggled with him and pleaded with him to stop. I should have fought harder to restrain him.' The man looked down into his lap and shook his head.

'You must not blame yourself,' said his brother.

'Please,' said Dr Harker gently. 'What happened then?'

'Well,' said the clockmaker, looking up, 'my fellow passenger shouted at the fiend who had attacked us and stood his ground bravely, refusing to give up any of his valuables. He pulled the pistol from his coat pocket and fired it straight at the brigand. Straight at him . . .'

'Yes?' said Dr Harker.

'Well . . . I . . . the highwayman simply sat there unharmed.' A murmur rippled round the customers.

'The man missed?' said Dr Harker.

'Yes . . . No . . . I do not see how he could have missed so completely,' said the clockmaker. 'But in any case, as our fellow passenger stood there, with the smoke still rising from his pistol, the highwayman suddenly—' He broke off and stared ahead, trying to come to terms with the memory.

'What is it?' asked Dr Harker.

'He . . . he . . .' continued the clockmaker, as if in a trance. 'He suddenly pointed at our fellow – merely pointed, mark you – and the American emitted a

strangled cry and a scream, and then to our amazement a glow began to emanate from his body and he
dropped to the ground. Smoke seemed to be rising
from his chest. His eyes were open and staring.' He
looked around the coffee house at the faces of his
listeners and said quietly, almost to himself. 'He . . .
was . . . dead.'

Tom looked at Dr Harker for some comfort, but
the doctor's face was as inscrutable as ever. Thornley's
face too was mask-like. How could a man be killed in
such a manner? Tom wondered. How could someone
be killed merely by the pointing of a finger? There
was no reason to doubt the man's story. There were
other witnesses, after all.

'What happened then?' asked Dr Harker.

'Then?' said the clockmaker, surprised by the
question and wondering how much more of a tale Dr
Harker wanted.

'Did the highwayman speak again?'

'Yes,' he replied. 'The fiend shouted at us
triumphantly that the same fate would befall anyone
who did not obey him immediately. You may not be
surprised to learn that we co-operated most readily
after that. We are not brave men, sir. We are not fighting men.'

'There is no shame in being robbed,' said Dr
Harker. 'Or in choosing to live.'

'The rider came closer and threw a sack into the

carriage for us to fill and we all did so with a fearful energy. He reached out for the sack and I handed it back to him. I saw eyes twinkle in what had seemed empty sockets as he took it from me. He then bellowed for us to move on. I looked at the lifeless form of my fellow on the ground, but to my shame we left him there. Forgive me, Lord.'

'Try not to judge yourself too harshly,' said Dr Harker. 'There is nothing you could have done. We should all have done the same in your place.' Gentlemen around the room nodded in agreement.

'Thank you, sir,' said the clockmaker, smiling weakly. 'And I must own that I am not a total wretch in this regard. I did seek out the sheriff when we reached Camden and rode with him and his men to the spot where the attack had taken place.'

'Good man,' said Dr Harker. 'And so you were able to take the body back. Were you able to discover who the poor man was?'

'But that's just it,' he answered. 'He wasn't there.'

'Wasn't there? Could you have been mistaken about the location?'

'No,' said the clockmaker. 'There was a milestone next to the carriage where the man fell. There can be no doubt that that was the place. But there was no sign of the body.'

'Perhaps some passer-by found it?' suggested Dr

Harker.

'Perhaps.' The clockmaker opened his mouth to continue, but a strange high-pitched whine suddenly screeched out and everyone winced and turned to look for its source.

Reverend Purney from Newgate prison was rubbing his bony finger round the rim of his brandy glass. ' "And I looked, and behold a pale horse," ' he quoted. ' "And his name that sat upon him was Death, and Hell followed with him. And power was given unto them over the fourth part of the earth, to kill with sword, and with hunger, and with death, and with the beasts of the earth." Revelations, chapter six, verse eight.'

'Do you honestly believe that the end of the world will be signalled by a highwayman?' said Dr Harker. 'Really, Purney. You seem to be positively eager for the Apocalypse.'

'These are strange times,' replied Purney. 'Did you not see the strange lights in the sky? Does the Lord not give us signs and wonders? Is the country not crawling with papists? Do you not wish to be prepared for the second coming? All your clever words will be of little consequence on the Day of Judgement, Doctor. "Blessed is he that watcheth, and keepeth his garments, lest he walk naked, and they see his shame." Revelations, chapter sixteen, verse fifteen. Perhaps you need to read your Bible a little more and your science books a little less.'

Dr Harker shook his head and turned back to the clockmaker, who was already getting up to leave. The doctor stood and shook his hand. 'It was good to meet you, sir,' he said. 'I hope these events do not trouble you long.'

'Thank you, sir,' he replied. 'You have been very kind.' He bowed and put on his hat. The clockmaker's brother got up too, shook his head and patted Dr Harker on the arm before making for the door.

Tom looked around the room and saw the customers turn back to their coffees and newspapers: all except for Purney, who continued to scowl at Dr Harker as if trying to bring the wrath of the Almighty down on him that instant.

'Quite a tale,' said Thornley, whose eyes were completely closed now.

'You do not believe him?' said Dr Harker.

'I neither believe nor disbelieve him. He does not concern me. Frankly, Josiah, I am a little surprised at the interest you take in these people.'

'I thought you took an interest in everything,' said Dr Harker. Thornley smiled. 'You never did say why you were here, Daniel.'

Thornley opened his eyes and leaned forward. 'I am here to help you, Josiah, if you'll let me. But first I need you to stop playing games with me.' He looked at Tom and then back to his friend. 'You said earlier that you had had no visitors but that is untrue.' Dr

Harker said nothing. 'You were visited by a mutual friend of ours. Please do not deny it, because I know it to be true.'

'Then why ask? It seems to me that it is you who are playing games. And I am not aware of needing your help.'

'That,' said Thornley, getting to his feet, 'is precisely why you do.' With that he tipped his hat to them both, smiled his wide bright smile and left.

Tom looked at Dr Harker, but the doctor seemed to be in a world of his own. Above the clatter and clink of the coffee house, Tom heard Purney mutter, as if to himself: ' "And his name that sat upon him was Death." '

6

# A VISITOR *from* AMERICA

It was a troubled Tom Marlowe who entered the churchyard of St Bride's on a cool March morning a week or so later. He was still plagued by seemingly unanswerable questions, and Dr Harker was being as inscrutable as ever.

'I wish I could talk to you, Will,' said Tom. 'Really talk to you. Dr Harker has said I mustn't say anything about the things I've seen, but I can't just pretend I never saw them. For a start, who is Monsieur Petit and why was he pretending to be French when I'm sure he was Scottish?' The cherub on Will's headstone looked back with its usual blank smile. 'And who is Daniel Thornley? How does Dr Harker know him? Something is going on, I'm sure of it . . . but what?'

Tom dropped onto his haunches so that he was level with the cherub and reached out his hand to rest on the cold stone above its carved curls.

'Oh, Will,' said Tom with a sigh. 'What shall I do? All this secrecy is choking me. Besides, suppose Dr Harker is in trouble and needs my help but won't ask?' This last thought seemed to stir him into action. 'I've got to talk to someone, Will, but who? Who can I trust?'

Tom stood up and snapped his fingers. 'Of course! Ocean! If there's any man in London I can trust, it's him. Ocean will know what to do! Thanks, Will.'

With that, Tom walked briskly towards the church-yard gate and headed off towards the Lamb and Lion printing house.

'Ocean,' said Tom. 'How are you?'

'Me?' said Ocean without looking up from the pamphlets he was sorting. 'I'm fine. How's everything going with Dr Harker? Is he teaching you everything he knows, then?'

'Actually, Ocean, it's about Dr Harker that I've come,' said Tom. 'You see—'

'Tom,' said Mr Marlowe, who had just appeared in

the doorway with another man, who was dressed in expensive clothes. 'I . . . I wasn't expecting you.'

'Tom!' said the other man.

'Excuse me,' said Tom. 'Do I know you?'

'Does he know me?' said the stranger, turning to Mr Marlowe, whose face bore a strange, heavy expression Tom had never seen before. 'Does he know me indeed?' The man turned back to Tom. 'It is to my shame that you do not know me, Tom. Had I been a better man, you should have known me well, but what's done is dead and I say best bury it and be done. I'm here now and that's the news, eh, lad? All the way from America.'

'I'm sorry—' began Tom, utterly perplexed.

'Sorry? You? Sorry? Why, there's no need for you to feel sorry. There's only one in this room that needs use of that word, eh, Marlowe, and that's the man you see before you now, but I say, what use is all the sorrys in purgatory if you don't make amends, eh, lad? I could stand in the pillory for days, Tom – weeks, even, but it wouldn't make things right, now would it?'

'Make what right?' Tom asked. 'Who are you, sir?'

The man stopped with his mouth wide open, looked first at Tom, then at Mr Marlowe, then back to Tom, before slapping his palm against his forehead. 'But of course. I was forgetting that Mr Marlowe here – fine upstanding man that he is—'

'Be careful, Greaves . . .' began Mr Marlowe ominously.

'Who is this man, Father?' said Tom, seeing the anxiety growing on Mr Marlowe's face.

'Ah, but isn't that just the nut of it, Tom? Haven't you just put your finger right there on it?' said the man with a grin. 'The man there,' he said, pointing to Mr Marlowe; 'that man there, he's not your father at all, lad.'

Tom looked at Mr Marlowe in disbelief, but Mr Marlowe said nothing to contradict it. He looked at Tom with tears filling his eyes but kept his peace.

'And you might ask how come I know these facts pertaining to your good self, Tom,' said the man. 'Well,' he went on, 'the short of it is that I know that he ain't your father because *I* am. I am your father, Tom, and right proud to be finally making your acquaintance.'

The man held out his hand for Tom to shake, but Tom looked at Ocean, who stood as if in a trance, and then at Mr Marlowe, who opened his mouth to speak – but whatever words he hoped would come failed to arrive and he closed his lips again and screwed his eyes shut. When he opened them again, Tom was gone.

Tom wandered out into the street and walked like a blind man, shoving his way through the crowd, oblivious to the complaints and curses. He didn't think about where he was going; he didn't think about much at all. His mind was numb, as if the blow of hearing that news had deadened it.

Suddenly, like a rush of wind, the sound of the world around him came flooding back in. Tom looked around like a sleepwalker, waking to find himself in Smithfield Market. Cattle were lowing, sheep bleating, pigs grunting and a cart full of chickens in wicker cages rumbled by spraying a shower of feathers in its wake.

Mr Marlowe had closed up the shop but Ocean let him in. Ocean patted him on the back but neither of them said a word, and Tom climbed the stairs to find Mr Marlowe seated at the old oak table; the table he had eaten at every day of his life until his move to Dr Harker's house.

'Tom!' said Mr Marlowe, rising a little unsteadily to his feet. 'I thought . . . I don't know what I thought, son.'

'Don't call me that!' snapped Tom.

'Tom! I've lied to you, I know, but I only ever did what I thought was best.'

'How could it be best for you to pretend you were my father? To tell me how you loved my mother? Who are you?'

'I'm your uncle, lad,' said Mr Marlowe. 'Your uncle. And I did love your mother. More than anything in the world. She was my sister. My dear sweet sister, and there's not a day goes by when I don't miss her. Not everything was a lie.'

'Not everything?' shouted Tom. 'I have called you Father for as long as I can remember and now I find you're my uncle, and you say not everything is a lie. Well, it feels like it to me!'

'I'm sorry, Tom,' said Mr Marlowe. 'You don't understand—'

'Then make me understand,' said Tom coldly. 'For I dearly wish to learn.'

Mr Marlowe motioned for him to sit and, after a moment's delay, Tom sat down and his uncle sat opposite him. Mr Marlowe drew the flats of both palms down his face, as if he were wiping away sweat. Tom had seen that gesture a thousand times before; seen those huge hands etched with ingrained ink that no amount of scrubbing would ever get out.

'Oh, Tom,' said Mr Marlowe with a sigh. 'I don't know where to begin.' He looked at Tom but Tom said nothing. 'I was six years older than your mother. Our parents died of smallpox when I was only ten, and Jane and me we were sent to the workhouse school. They were tough times, Tom, but me and your mother, we looked out for each other and we got through.

'Even in a place like that, there's sometimes kindness, and there was a lady that used to come and visit and her husband ran a printing house and one day she said would I like to come and be apprenticed there? Would I like to be apprenticed? Oh, Tom, it was like a dream come true. And Jane came too, of course, and the lady said she could be a maid.

'And that's what happened. That's what we did. I worked there as happy as anyone might, and a better master or mistress a body never could have found. Jane and me, so long without any happiness, were now as happy as sunshine.' Mr Marlowe looked at Tom's face and saw that the coldness of his expression had not melted even with the warmth of these memories. He realized he ought to speed his tale along.

'So, anyway, the years passed and I worked through my apprenticeship and Mr Godfrey asked me to stay and work on at his printing house, an offer I gladly accepted. And things might have continued that way, had your mother not met . . . not met your father.' Mr Marlowe gave Tom another glance, but Tom remained expressionless.

'All of a sudden, there he was – your father, Nathaniel Greaves. For the life of me, Tom, I can't recall where and how your mother ever met the man, for she was rarely out of my sight and I had got into the habit of looking out for her since the workhouse days. But meet him she did, curse it all. Meet him she did.' Mr Marlowe stopped and suddenly smiled at the thought that had just come to him. 'Of course, Tom, if she hadn't met him, you'd not be here, so there's good in everything.'

Tom stared on as if in a trance.

'Anyway, in no time at all Jane is saying he wants to marry her and that she loves him, and what could I do? He came round, all proper like, and spoke to me and my master and mistress and told us all how he was an engraver and how he had great prospects. He was a charmer all right. Thing is, Tom, he really *was* an engraver, and a fine one at that. If he had put the effort into that that he put into . . . into other matters . . . he would have been someone.

'Him and Jane got married and I was happy for her, though I was sad to see her go. I shook your father's hand and told him to take good care of her and he swore he would. Swore it on the Bible there in the church, curse him. Then you were born, Tom, and Jane was so happy. I never saw her so happy as when she held you. But Greaves – your father – he was already breaking his oath . . .' Mr Marlowe slammed his hand down on the table. 'No, Tom, it ain't right. It's not for me to tell you this. Greaves should tell you himself.' He got up and made for the door.

Tom didn't know what to do or where to go. Mr Marlowe stopped for a moment and turned back. 'Greaves said he would wait for you,' he said. 'He's staying at The Eagle.'

# 7

# Nathaniel GREAVES

Tom walked into the brick-paved courtyard of
The Eagle. It was deserted except for two
mangy cats, who were squaring up to fight until Tom
appeared and now ran off in opposite directions,
shooting nervous glances over their shoulders as they
went. Greaves called down from the gallery that ran
all around the courtyard, supported by carved
wooden posts.

'Up here, Tom,' he said. 'Glad you decided to
come!'

Tom climbed the stairs and Greaves showed him to his room, where he saw a jug of beer and two pewter mugs on a side table.

'Sit yourself down, Tom,' Greaves said. 'I suppose Marlowe has been painting my portrait in all its boils and wrinkles?'

'Actually,' said Tom, 'he said that it was up to you to tell me what I needed to know.'

Greaves raised an eyebrow and then laughed a bitter laugh. He poured them both a beer. 'Did he now? Did he? So he told you nothing then?'

'Nothing,' replied Tom. 'Though he made it plain he did not like you.'

Greaves laughed again. 'Well, nothing's changed in that regard,' he said. 'But I suppose he's right, old Marlowe. I suppose you deserve some history. What is it that you'd like to know? Anything at all, lad. Ask me anything you like. We've got a lot of catching up to do, eh, lad?'

'Why did you go?' asked Tom coldly. 'If you are my father, why did you leave?'

'Cut straight to the bone, don't you, boy?' said Greaves with a smile.

'Why did you leave?' Tom repeated.

'Tom!' said Greaves, clenching his fist. 'Do you think I don't feel a devil's crop of shame for leaving you, boy? Do you think I don't wish I could change things? Do you think I wouldn't like to wipe those sins away?' He looked into Tom's eyes; Tom could not hold his gaze and looked away.

'I was a different man then, Tom. I was a hard man and a weak man. But things is different now. Life has shoved me in its furnace and beat me on its anvil and I'm a changed man. It near broke me, Tom, but I come out stronger for it. And I come to make amends.'

'How can you?' said Tom. 'I've been brought up with lies, and all because you left. And you still haven't told me why!'

'Ah, Tom,' said Greaves. 'You probably won't understand. Look at you. Fine upstanding lad like you. You don't need to have dreams.'

'Dreams?'

'Yeah, dreams. Old Marlowe could never understand why I wanted more than this.' Greaves waved his hand round at the whole London scene. 'Me, I used to look at them ships in the dock and wonder where they'd been and if I'd ever see anything but the inside of these city walls and the stinking Thames. You ever felt like that, Tom?'

'Yes,' said Tom, for he had felt like that very often. 'But I would never leave my wife and baby.'

Greaves smiled. 'Be careful what you say you'll never do, Tom. You might surprise yourself one day.'

'And is that what you did?' asked Tom. 'Surprise yourself?'

'Look, Tom. What do you want me to say? I was a wretch. Where a good man would have seen a beautiful wife and baby, I saw my coffin. I saw my life stretched out, nailed up, finished. I was a fool.'

'So it's my fault that you left?'

'No, Tom!' said Greaves. 'Now I didn't say that. It was me at fault. There was nothing but good in you and your mother.' He glanced away and sighed, and then looked back at Tom. 'I fell in with ill company. I took to drinking more than is wise and spending more money than I had. The business began to fail as I did less and less work. And the less I worked the more I drank and the more I spent. Well, anyway, the long and the short of it is that I went from bad to worse and became the kind of wretch a lad like you would cross the street to avoid.'

'And what about us?' said Tom. 'What happened to my mother and me?'

'It came so that I barely saw you, Tom. Even in the state I was in, I could not bear the shame. And not because your mother chided me, but because she never did. Through it all she only ever saw the good in me. Old Marlowe saw straight through me, curse him, but she would have none of it. She was all good-ness, Tom, and if there was any good in me at all, she was the only one as could see it.'

'But you left her all the same. And me too.'

Greaves looked at Tom with tears in his eyes.

'You've a hard heart, Tom,' he said. 'But I dare say that's my doing too.'

'Why America?' Tom asked. 'Why go so far?'

Greaves sighed and took another drink. 'So Marlowe really did not tell you then?'

'He told me nothing,' said Tom. 'I wish someone would.'

'I was transported, Tom,' Greaves told him. 'I was a convicted felon, lucky not to hang, if the truth be known.'

'Convicted? Convicted of what?'

'Thievery,' replied Greaves. 'I was as poor a thief as I was a husband and father and got caught too easily. My only luck was in having my trial before a soft-hearted or soft-headed judge who saw fit to spare me the noose. In its stead he sent me to slave in the tobacco fields of the Americas. Your mother came to see me off on the quayside as we were taken aboard, with you in her arms. I thought I would die of shame as I shuffled along in those manacles and chains, Tom. I cursed myself for the weak man I was and for the trail of pain I left in my wake.

'And so I left London for the first time in my life and sailed across the sea to Annapolis in the place they call Maryland. Imagine it, Tom: me, who had never been further than the other side of the Thames.'

'But did you never try to keep in contact? We were your family, after all.'

'No,' replied Greaves. 'I felt it was better that I died out there and your mother might forget me and marry again and you might have a father to be proud of. Of course, your mother, bless her dear heart, she stayed faithful and true to me and only ever hoped that I might return. But at least I was not around to drag you down with me, Tom.'

'Are you trying to say I was better off for having you leave?' asked Tom.

'Yes,' said Greaves. 'I suppose I am. With me out of the way, Marlowe could step in and interfere as much as he'd always wanted to.'

'Without his "interference" we would have ended up in the poorhouse,' said Tom.

'True enough. But that's my point. Marlowe did a better job of bringing you up than I ever could, and that's just how it is. I was no good to you then, Tom.'

'And why should you be any good to me now?' said Tom.

'I'm your father, Tom,' said Greaves.

'You were my father then.'

Greaves looked down at the tabletop and when he looked back at Tom there were tears in his eyes. 'I worked hard in those tobacco fields, Tom. Harder than I needed to. And the owner, Mr Bellingham, noticed the effort I put in. He gave me responsibility over other slaves, even though he knew I was a thief myself. He trusted me – though he had every reason not to. It was a kindness I never would forget.' Greaves paused, clearly moved by the memory. 'Then one day a letter come from Marlowe telling me your mother had died. I felt I was damned, Tom. All that lay ahead was the gates of Hell and any torments I might face there would be well deserved.'

'But you didn't come back,' said Tom.

'I couldn't, Tom. If I had come back before my time, I'd have been hanged.'

'But your time came to an end and you still didn't come back.'

'True, Tom,' said Greaves. 'Don't imagine I didn't think about you, because I did. But Marlowe had told me he was looking after you. I knew you were all right. And when my time was up Bellingham asked me to stay and paid me wages. Things were better how they were.'

'For you,' said Tom.

'I can't change the past, Tom.' Greaves sighed. 'What's done is done. I can only do something about the here and now and the years to come. I'm a different man. I'm not the man who left you. Won't you give me a chance?'

'To do what?' asked Tom.

'To try and make amends,' said Greaves.

'How? Why have you even come back? What have you got to offer me after all these years?'

'A chance to get out of this heaving ant hill and

come with me to America. A chance to see something better than the other side of the street.'

Tom looked at him and Greaves grinned. 'America?' said Tom. 'But . . .'

'I'm a wealthy man, Tom,' said Greaves. 'I dreamed my dream. When Bellingham died he left me land and then . . . Well, it doesn't matter how; the long and the short of it is I've made my fortune and I want you to share it with me. What do you say?'

# 8

# *The* TOMAHAWK

The afternoon sunshine filtered into the study, lighting up the floating specks of dust as Dr Harker lifted down boxes from cupboards and searched shelves for books. Tom opened up the ledger and turned to the page showing the last entry. He smoothed it down and picked up his pen.

'I saw Mr Marlowe yesterday, Tom,' said Dr Harker nonchalantly as he rummaged around in a large wooden chest.

'I'd rather not talk about it,' said Tom. 'If you don't

mind, sir.'

'No, Tom. Of course, of course. And how is everything going with Mr Greaves? It must have been—'

'With all respect, sir,' said Tom, a little more force-
fully than he had intended. 'These things are private.
We all have things that are private, don't we, sir?'

Dr Harker looked long and hard at Tom. He could
hear the tone in his voice and the hurt there too, but
he did not respond to it. He knew Tom's temper and
was happy to drop the subject. 'As you like, Tom. Back
to work then.'

The doctor picked up a large package wrapped in
calico and tied with string. 'I think you will find this
interesting. A friend of mine sent it to me from
Maine.' He pulled the string and the calico fell away
to reveal a small hatchet with a metal blade inscribed
with geometric designs set into a wooden handle
with black feathers tied to the shaft. He picked it up.
'It's an Indian tomahawk, Tom. Iroquois probably. It's
rather wonderful, is it not?'

Tom agreed that it was rather wonderful, though
he doubted it would be quite so appealing in the
hands of its original owner.

'Could you run downstairs, Tom,' asked the doctor,
'and ask Mrs Tibbs for a cloth and maybe a little
vinegar and we can see if we might clean this up a
little?'

Tom was almost at the bottom of the stairs when

there was an odd sound at the front door: a strange scratching and tapping. He drew the bolt and opened the door and to his horror found himself inches away from a face that was horribly beaten and bruised, with dried blood across the forehead and fresh blood streaming from the nose and lip. One of the eyes was closed behind blue and swollen lids. It took Tom a few seconds before he realized it was Daniel Thornley.

The door had been the only thing holding Thornley up, and now he slumped across the threshold and fell to the floor. Sarah came out from dusting the dining room and screamed, running to the kitchen for Mrs Tibbs, the housekeeper, and bringing Dr Harker down from his study.

'Dr Harker!' shouted Tom. 'Come quickly!'

Sarah reappeared, clutching a handkerchief to her face.

'Close the door, Sarah,' said Dr Harker as he crossed the hall, but Sarah did not move. 'Come, girl,' he urged, kindly but firmly. 'Be brave, now.'

Sarah inched her way past the fallen Thornley and closed the door.

'Now, Tom; help me here. Let's get him to the kitchen.' As they lifted him up Dr Harker asked, 'Can you walk, Daniel?'

'I think so, yes,' said Thornley, before hissing in pain. 'Who did this?'

'Could I – Aaah! – Could I trouble you for a

brandy, Josiah?' asked Thornley as they eased him into a seat.

'Sarah, fetch a bottle of brandy, will you? Mrs Tibbs, could I trouble you for a bowl of hot water and some linen?'

'Yes, Dr Harker, sir,' said Sarah, now restored to her usual efficient self. She brushed into Thornley as she left the room and he yelled after her, cursing loudly.

'I apologize for my friend here, ladies,' said Dr Harker. 'He is in some pain.'

'Of course, sir,' said Mrs Tibbs, tutting to herself.

'Now.' Dr Harker held a candle up in front of Thornley's face and inspected his injuries. 'Off with your waistcoat and shirt, man, and let's see what's amiss.'

Sarah shrieked again when she came in and saw Thornley stripped to the waist. She put down the brandy and hurried out of the room, blushing. Thornley was covered in red marks.

'Will you stop that infernal shrieking, you silly girl!' he shouted.

'I'll thank you not to talk to Sarah like that, Daniel. You will be black and blue on the morrow, but there does not appear to be anything broken. You must stay here for the next few days. You are a lucky man.'

Thornley laughed a wry laugh and instantly regretted it as he clenched his teeth in pain. 'Much more of this good fortune and I'll be a dead man,' he said.

Sarah reappeared with the bowl of hot water and left as hurriedly as before.

'Pour us all a drink, would you, Tom?' asked Dr Harker. 'And Daniel here will tell us what happened this evening.'

Tom poured the drinks and Thornley settled back in the chair, wincing again.

'Who did this to you, Daniel?' the doctor asked again.

Picking up his glass, Thornley cast a quick glance at Tom. 'Can we talk in private? No offence, young man, but my life hangs in the balance here, as you can see. It has nothing to do with you, I promise you. I simply do not know you, and this is too serious to rest on politeness.'

Dr Harker looked at Tom and Tom could see what was coming. 'I am sorry, Tom,' said the doctor. 'I must ask you to leave. It is for your own good.'

'Is it?' said Tom sharply. 'Never mind. I'll go. If you don't trust me—'

'Tom!'

But Tom was already in the hall and reaching for the front door. He wrenched it open and looked out at the courtyard. The earlier sunshine had been replaced by thick grey clouds and torrential rain. It was then he realized he had forgotten his coat and would have the embarrassment of going back to fetch it.

He slammed the door and then tiptoed across the hall to collect his coat from the hook by the stairs, hoping that Dr Harker and Thornley would not hear him. He did not want to talk to either of them. He just wanted to get out of the house as quickly as possible. As he edged past the door to the kitchen, he heard Dr Harker's voice.

'Who did this?'

Tom held his breath to hear the answer.

'It is best we do not talk about it, Josiah,' said Thornley. 'You know my life. You know the dangers. The less you know of this specific incident the better.'

'But surely—' began Dr Harker.

'I must insist. Secrecy is everything in my trade. Perhaps it would be better if I left—'

'Be still, Daniel,' said Dr Harker calmly. 'You are going nowhere in that condition.'

'I will be fine, Josiah,' said Thornley. 'There is something far more pressing to attend to.'

'And what is that?'

'They have McGregor,' Thornley replied.

Tom craned nearer at the sound of the name McGregor. So it was true. Dr Harker was somehow mixed up with the Scots. But was this McGregor a Jacobite?

'Jamie?' said Dr Harker. 'When?'

'Yesterday. He was arrested and taken to Newgate.

He is in the Red Room awaiting his fate. He'll hang for sure unless we help him.'

Tom had to stop himself gasping when he heard this. So it was true. Dr Harker and Mr Thornley were trying to aid a Jacobite. Tom wondered if this Jamie McGregor was the Monsieur Petit he had met.

'But how can we help him now?' asked Dr Harker.

'I have arranged it so that when Jamie is taken out of the Red Room to be interrogated, he will break free from his guards and escape. I was able to persuade the turnkeys that he is a spy working for the British government, and with the encouragement of a little cash, they were happy to play along. Once out he will need money.'

'How much?'

'A lot,' said Thornley. 'He must get out of the country and join his fellow exiles on the Continent. He will be safe there. A hundred pounds should do the job.'

'I will get the money first thing tomorrow,' said Dr Harker.

'Splendid,' said Thornley.

'Do you think Jamie can get away safely?' asked Dr Harker.

'If any of them can, he can. But I fear he will never be able to return, Josiah.'

'I agree, Daniel,' said Dr Harker. 'How do I get the money to him.'

'With all due respect, I think this rather lies within my area of expertise—'

'No, Daniel,' interrupted Dr Harker. 'You have done enough and risked enough. You have already done far more than anyone had a right to expect. I will deliver the money.'

'Be reasonable, Josiah,' said Thornley. 'The risks I have taken, I have taken willingly. I thank you for your concern, but I really think—'

'I must insist,' said Dr Harker. 'My mind is made up on the matter. Besides, if Jamie is to leave these shores then I would like to see him one last time.'

'Very well,' said Thornley reluctantly. 'I must respect your wishes in this, I suppose, as you are providing the money—'

'Indeed. Now what is the plan?'

'The plan?' said Thornley, hesitating slightly. 'The plan – yes, of course. Jamie's escape will be effected two days from now, on Thursday evening,' he said. 'He will leave Newgate under cover of darkness and go straight to the rendezvous point. You will need to ride north that night, out of London on the Hampstead Road. You will pass a stables and blacksmith's forge on your left; about a mile after that there is a blasted oak beside the road near to a barn. That is where Jamie will be waiting.'

Tom inched away and tiptoed out of the front door, taking as much time as he dared to close it as silently as possible. He hurried through the courtyard and out into Fleet Street, his mind reeling. There could be no doubt now: Dr Harker was at the very least helping a member of the Jacobite cause. At worst he was a Jacobite himself.

# 9

# T*he* TOWER Menagerie

**T**om saw Nathaniel Greaves in the distance as he walked towards the Stocks Market. He was still having great difficulty seeing this stranger as his father. Greaves had his back to Tom; he stood at the foot of the statue of Charles II, listening to a fiddler. Tom tapped him on the shoulder and he looked round and grinned, but turned back to the fiddler, clapping his hands to the tune. A small boy came up to them holding a battered pewter dish and Greaves tossed a few shining coins into it. The boy smiled and the fiddler shouted, 'Thank you, sir! You're a gentleman, sir!'

'You're very generous,' said Tom as they walked away.

Greaves shrugged. 'I can afford to be,' he said. 'And I love a bit of music.' He took a lungful of London air and spread out his arms as if about to break into song. 'I'm very glad to have your company,' he went on. 'Very glad.'

'I'm glad you're glad,' said Tom.

'Have you thought any more about my offer?'

'Yes,' replied Tom. 'I have thought about it a lot.'

'And have you reached any decision?'

'No. No, I haven't.'

'Well, that's a relief!' said Greaves.

'How so?' asked Tom.

'I thought you'd turn me down flat,' said Greaves. Tom smiled. 'So,' his father continued, 'I thought we might go on a little excursion, you and me.'

'An excursion?' said Tom. 'Where?'

Greaves whistled and waved at the driver of a hackney carriage; it rumbled up the street and came to a halt beside them.

'Come on, Tom,' said Greaves. 'Get in.'

'Where to, friend?' asked the cab driver.

'The Tower!' Greaves shut the door behind them and the driver flicked the reins. The cab jerked forward, rattling down the cobbles towards the river.

# T*he* TOWER Menagerie

'The Tower?' said Tom, the image of Lord Derwentwater's severed head making an unwelcome reappearance in his mind.

'Yeah,' said Greaves. 'I thought we might go to see the lions. That's if you want to.'

'Yes. Of course.' Tom hadn't been to the Menagerie for ages. The last time he had been was with Will. It was one of the few times that Tom had ever seen Will stand still or remain silent for any length of time. Tom had smiled at him as they stood in front of the animals and assumed it was a sense of wonder that had struck Will dumb, but when his friend turned, Tom saw tears in his eyes. They had left soon after and Will had barely spoken all the way back to Fleet Street. Tom never asked him what had upset him, and Will never mentioned it.

'And it's not just any old day down at the Menagerie,' said Greaves, searching his pockets. 'Look here!' He held out a card for Tom to read. It was an invitation to the Tower Menagerie to see the lions being washed in the moat. It had a crudely drawn illustration of a wide-eyed lion on it. 'What about that, then? That ought to be something to see, eh, Tom?'

Tom smiled and raised his eyebrows.

'What?' his father asked.

'It's a joke.'

'A joke?' said Greaves. 'What do you mean?'

'The lions being washed,' said Tom. 'It's a joke. It's April the first.'

'Well I'll be . . .' said Greaves.

'They do it every year. They only really catch foreigners now, because everyone in London is already in the know.'

Greaves shook his head and grinned. 'Foreigners, eh? Well, I suppose I am a foreigner now, in a way. What a chub! All Fools' Day. I must be getting old.' Then he laughed and threw the card out of the carriage window. 'So how come you ain't working for old Marlowe any more?' he asked.

'It's a long story,' said Tom.

'Long, or you just don't want to tell it?'

Tom smiled.

'And this Dr Harker fellow,' his father went on. 'You're his apprentice, are you?'

'Not exactly,' said Tom.

'Not exactly? Strikes me you either is or you ain't. And what trade is he teaching you anyway?'

'It's a bit late for you to take such a concern in my upbringing, don't you think?' said Tom. 'I believe you were once an engraver by trade.'

Greaves raised his hands in mock surrender. 'That's fair, Tom,' he admitted. 'I've got no right to poke and pry.'

'No,' said Tom. 'You haven't.' But he smiled. He wanted to remain angry at Greaves but he found himself liking him despite himself. 'I'm just finding it hard to make sense of all this. A few weeks ago I knew who I was and now I find I wasn't that person at all.'

'It ain't you that's changed, Tom,' said Greaves. 'And from what little I know there ain't no need for you to change neither. I got no right to take any credit for you – I wish I could – but from what I see you're a fine lad.'

'Tower!' shouted the driver as the carriage slowed down and stopped.

Greaves paid the fare and Tom took in the view. Though the clouds out to the east were almost black, the sun now shone where they stood, and lit up the battlements in front of them, and the White Tower beyond. They walked down towards the entrance, paid their money at the gate and walked across the moat to the Menagerie.

There were various animals there, but like most people Tom and his father made straight for the lions. When they got to the dens, Greaves wafted his hand in front of his nose.

'It stinks as bad as Fleet prison in here,' he said, and it was true that the smell of animal dung, damp straw and the offal that had recently been thrown into the dens was overpowering even by London standards. 'I'm sure these brutes were livelier the last time I saw them. But then, we've all got a bit older, I suppose.'

'They look sad,' said Tom, looking at one of the

lions stretched out on the floor, his eyes half closed. A fly landed on the lion's nose and crawled across it but the lion did not stir.

'Sad or not,' said Greaves with a smile, 'that flea-ridden bag of bones would happily rip you to pieces if you went in there, and that's for sure.' The lion slumped over and closed his eyes, dozing. 'Hmmm. Well, when he wakes up, maybe.' He tapped the bars but the lion did not move. 'It makes you think, though, doesn't it?'

'What does?' asked Tom.

'Well,' said his father, 'the old story that if one of the lions dies then the king will die. You've heard that, haven't you?'

'Yes. Of course.'

'Well then,' said Greaves, dropping his voice to a whisper as an elderly couple passed by. 'If they shot one of these lions they could solve this Jacobite non-sense at a stroke, couldn't they? All we'd have to do is wait and see whether it was George or the Pretender that followed suit. Though I have to confess, Tom, I couldn't care less either way.'

'Do you mind if we go?' asked Tom.

'Mind? Why would I mind?'

'I'm sorry,' said Tom. 'I've spoiled your excursion.'

Greaves smiled and put his hand on Tom's shoulder. 'Nonsense,' he said. 'I've got you for company now, haven't I? You're a sensitive lad, Tom.

To tell the truth, seeing all these bars is bringing back a few unpleasant memories.'

'Yes,' said Tom. 'I've been in Newgate myself.'

His father stared at him in amazement.

'As a visitor!' said Tom, laughing.

'Thank goodness for that!' said Greaves. 'I thought there was a criminal career that you'd forgotten to mention.'

Tom laughed again. 'No,' he said. 'It was last year, during my adventure with Dr Harker and Ocean . . . and the Mohawk Tonsahoten.'

'Ah yes . . . The famous Death and the Arrow murders,' said Greaves.

'You know about them?'

'Oh yes. I heard you was involved. The Boston papers even carried the story, you know. I was thinking I really ought to read Dr Harker's book. I dare say, though, he made it seem more exciting than it was.'

'No, no,' said Tom. 'It was really exciting. Terrifying sometimes too. Dr Harker is such an amazing man and you should see Ocean . . .' Tom trailed off.

'Yes?' prompted Greaves.

'Well,' said Tom, 'it was dangerous and frightening and everything, but I never felt so alive as in those days. I lost my best friend in Will and then along came Dr Harker and Ocean and they put their lives at risk to track down his killer. But now they . . .' He trailed off again.

'What is it, Tom?' asked his father.

'Well,' said Tom, 'it's not easy for me to talk to Ocean at the moment, what with him being at the Lamb and Lion . . . ' Greaves nodded. 'And I always felt Dr Harker trusted me, but now it seems like he doesn't. He doesn't trust me at all.'

'About what?' said Greaves.

Tom shook his head. 'I shouldn't say.'

'Well, you can't complain about Dr Harker not trusting you' – Greaves laughed – 'and then make it plain you don't trust me!'

Tom smiled. 'You're right. You're right. It's about time I told someone. But it mustn't go any further.'

Greaves put his hand to his heart. 'I swear, Tom.'

So Tom told his father about the executions on Tower Hill and about Daniel Thornley and about the Jacobite rebel pulled from the Thames and about Thornley's beating. He told him about Monsieur Petit and how he was really a Scotsman called McGregor. He told him how he had listened to the plan to break him out of Newgate and help him flee the country with the help of £100. And all through the telling, Greaves listened in silence until Tom had finished and then he breathed a great sigh.

'Well, Tom,' he said, 'that's quite a weight to have been carrying round. I'm glad you felt able to tell me, but if you don't mind me saying, I think this Dr Harker of yours is mixed up in something dark. Just leave it be, Tom, that's my advice. Dr Harker clearly doesn't want your help or he'd ask for it. I know the doctor is a friend of yours, but you need to think of yourself here. This could end at Tyburn.'

'I know,' said Tom. 'I just . . . I don't know.'

'I don't see that there's anything you can do, Tom.'

'I know, I know,' said Tom. 'But I don't know if I can carry on working for Dr Harker with all this going on.' He turned to his father. 'You won't tell anyone that I told you this, will you?'

'Course not, Tom. I know how to keep a secret,' said Greaves. 'Come on, let's walk back. It's been a while since I roamed my home town.'

'Yes,' said Tom with a smile. 'I'd like that.'

And so they did, Greaves pointing out all the sights as if Tom had never seen them before. He moaned at the condition of London Bridge and said that they should knock it down and start again. 'Nonsuch House looks like it'll fall down on its own before much longer!'

When they passed the Monument, Greaves turned to Tom. 'The Great Fire was the best thing that ever happened to London, if you ask me,' he commented. 'It's just a shame it didn't burn the rest of the place down with it. There's too much history here, Tom. Everyone's got their heads on backwards when they should look forwards.'

Tom smiled and wondered if this outburst hadn't

got more to do with his father's wish to wipe away his own history.

However, when they got to St Paul's Cathedral, Greaves looked up and whistled. 'None of this was here when I left, Tom,' he said. 'And now look at it. What do you say we don't go and take ourselves up to the top of that dome?'

Tom's face fell as he remembered the last time he had been up there and how he had nearly been thrown from the top. Nothing would have induced him to climb it again. 'I've already done it,' he said. 'It's nothing special.'

'Well, if you say so,' said his father. 'Mind you, I—'

'The White Rider robs again!' shouted a thin voice nearby. A sickly looking newspaper boy was standing among a knot of customers who muttered and tutted loudly.

'That's the highwayman Dr Harker was so interested in,' said Tom. 'Look, he robbed a coach near Hampstead two nights ago.'

Greaves looked about him and then took out his watch. 'Highwayman, do you say?' he said a little nervously. 'Will you look at the time, Tom! I had no idea it was so late.'

'Is everything all right?'

'All right?' Greaves repeated. 'Yes . . . Yes . . . Of course, Tom. No . . . I've just got some business to attend to. No rest for the wicked, eh?'

'I've enjoyed the time we've spent together,' said Tom.

'So have I,' said his father.

'The White Rider! The White Rider!' shouted the newspaper boy.

'Look, Tom, I've got to go,' said Greaves, slapping Tom on the shoulder and walking away backwards. 'I'll be in touch!' he called, and was soon lost in the crowd.

# 10

# JAMIE McGREGOR

D r Harker had not managed to get a single word out of his assistant beyond 'Good Morning' or the occasional 'Yes, sir' or 'No, sir' since the morning began. Tom was aware of the doctor's frustration but felt it served him right, given that he had been as tight-lipped as an oyster himself these past weeks.

'How was your day out with Mr Greaves?' asked Dr Harker, more brightly than he felt. 'Or is that private?' he added with a smile.

Tom did not return it. 'It was very enjoyable, thank

you, sir,' he said primly. 'My father has asked me to sail with him when he leaves.'

'Has he indeed?' said Dr Harker, trying to sound casual. 'And what have you said in response?'

'I have told him that I will think about it.'

'Good Lord,' said Dr Harker. 'Surely you would not give up everything you have here?'

'He is my father, sir,' said Tom. 'And it is a chance for me to see the world. He sails for Africa and then America. I want to have some adventures of my own, sir.'

'Yes, Tom,' said Dr Harker. 'Of course you do, and you shall, I'm sure. But still, you hardly know the man . . .'

'With all respect, sir,' said Tom, 'I hardly know you either, if it comes to that, but I would have trusted you with my life.'

'Would have?' said Dr Harker. 'Say what's on your mind, Tom.'

Tom hesitated.

'We're alone, Tom,' the doctor reassured him. 'Sarah and Mrs Tibbs are in the kitchen and Daniel is asleep in his room.'

'Well, sir,' said Tom, 'I mean that you have made it clear that you do not trust me and—'

'What makes you think I don't trust you, Tom?' asked Dr Harker. 'Whatever you know, or think you know, this was never a matter of trust. Why, I trust you as much as I trust myself. Honestly I do.'

'Then why shut me out, sir?' said Tom. 'I've been of help to you before. Maybe I can be again.'

'You have been a great help, Tom,' said Dr Harker. 'We have been through a lot and I hold you very dear. But that is why I have tried to protect you.'

'You need not,' said Tom. 'I know already, and your secret is safe with me, sir.'

Dr Harker raised an eyebrow and squinted at Tom a little. 'What do you know, Tom? *Exactly?*'

'Well, sir,' said Tom, dropping his voice to a whisper and quickly looking about him. 'Mr Thornley is a Jacobite and you and he are aiding another rebel, a Scotsman named McGregor.'

Dr Harker's expression became very grave. 'Have you told anyone of this suspicion?'

'No,' said Tom a little nervously, for Dr Harker had the same hard look he had witnessed on the way to the theatre.

'Tom,' said the doctor, 'this is important. Very important. Have you mentioned this suspicion to anyone at all?'

'I . . . That is . . . I might have said something to my father,' said Tom.

'Which one?'

'Well, both, as a matter of fact,' Tom admitted. Dr Harker put both hands over his face. 'Mr Marlowe thought it very amusing.'

'Did he?' said Dr Harker. 'I wish I could say the same. Did I not make it clear how dangerous it would be to speculate about these matters, Tom?'

'But I overheard you and Mr Thornley—'

'So you have been spying on me, Tom?'

'I had not meant to,' said Tom, blushing. 'Honestly, sir, I—'

'Never mind,' said Dr Harker with a sigh. 'The damage is done. And what of Mr Greaves? Did he think it was funny?'

'He didn't say,' said Tom. 'I'm sorry, sir. I needed to confide in someone and I haven't managed to speak to Ocean since . . . and you were behaving . . .'

'Well?'

'Suspiciously,' said Tom.

Dr Harker closed his eyes and leaned on his clasped hands as if in prayer. 'I am sorry, Tom. You are absolutely right,' he said. 'I *have* been behaving suspiciously. But tell me, what gave us away as being Jacobites?'

'Well,' said Tom, 'there was Monsieur Petit for a start.'

'Yes?' said Dr Harker.

'He was no Frenchman. I heard him speaking with a Scottish accent before I entered the room.'

Dr Harker chuckled. 'It was a poor ruse, Tom, but you are a clever lad to have seen through it all the same.'

'Then there was the night after the theatre,' said Tom. 'You knew so much about the murdered Jacobite and about the dagger – the skin—'

'Skean-dhu,' said Dr Harker.

'And I forgot to mention Tower Hill,' said Tom, growing in confidence. 'I saw tears in your eyes, Doctor.'

'You did,' Dr Harker agreed, nodding. 'You did.'

'And Mr Thornley,' said Tom. 'I believe that you and he are conspiring to help a Jacobite rebel – this man called Jamie McGregor – to escape this country and flee to the Continent to join the Pretender.'

Dr Harker smiled. 'You are a remarkably intelligent young man,' he said. 'Really you are. And you are correct in every regard—'

'So it *is* true!' said Tom.

'Except that I am not a Jacobite,' the doctor added. 'And neither is Daniel Thornley. In fact, quite the reverse in Daniel's case – Daniel is a government agent . . . a Jacobite *hunter*, Tom.'

Tom looked baffled. 'But how? . . . I . . . I don't understand, sir.'

'You have heard me mention my late wife?' said Dr Harker.

'Yes, many times. But I don't see what—'

'Mary was Scottish, Tom. That is how I came to know something of the ways of that country, and some of the language too.'

88

'I still don't understand,' said Tom.

'The man you met in my study is a Jacobite, Tom, just as you guessed. He is a Scotsman and not a Frenchman, just as you discovered for yourself, though he has lived in France in recent years. However, he is also my late wife's brother. His name is Jamie McGregor. It is he whom I am trying to aid. Not for his cause, but for the debt I owe to Mary's memory and, well, because however misguided I might believe him to be, Jamie is a fine man, and I would not see him die a traitor's death. That was why you saw tears, Tom, on Tower Hill. It was a tragic event, it's true, and tears were not out of place, but I cried for what might become of Jamie and what Mary would have felt had she been alive to see.'

'But you risk a traitor's death yourself, sir,' said Tom, 'aiding a Jacobite.'

'That I do, Tom. And that is why I wanted you to be at some distance from me. There is a kind of Bedlam fever at work in the country and there will be more deaths before this thing is finished. People are seeing Jacobites in every darkened corner.'

Tom smiled. 'Like me, I suppose.'

'No, Tom,' said Dr Harker. 'You used the evidence you saw to draw a perfectly logical conclusion. You simply did not have all the facts.'

'But why is Mr Thornley helping you?' said Tom. 'I

know he is an old friend, but why would he risk his life for Jamie?'

'Ah,' said Dr Harker. 'To answer that we need to go back many, many years to when we were both children, growing up some miles north of here, in Stoke Newington. Our parents were great friends and Daniel and I became inseparable. We went to school together. My father was a military man in his younger days and it was his fervent wish that I should live that life, but he had to accept that my interests lay elsewhere, just as I have had to accept that my own son has no interest in anything but the navy. He did, however, teach both Daniel and me to use a sword – something I have had cause to thank him for. Daniel and I would spend hours in combat with our wooden swords.' He smiled at the recollection. 'Then the McGregor family arrived, with young Jamie and his lovely sister Mary.'

'Your wife?' asked Tom.

'Yes. Though she was only a girl then. I fell in love with her on sight. And so did Daniel.'

'Did you fight over her?'

'No,' said Dr Harker. 'We loved each other too much. But something changed between us. We were drifting apart anyway. We both went away to university, but though we stayed in touch, something was happening to Daniel. He was becoming more and more politically minded and more and more ferociously anti-Catholic. He became involved in the rebellion of Monmouth in the West Country back in 'eighty-five. Do you know about that, Tom?'

'A little,' said Tom. 'Monmouth was the bas— the illegitimate son of Charles the Second, wasn't he? He was to be king instead of James the Second on account of James being Catholic. I know he was defeated and executed.'

'Yes, Tom,' said Dr Harker. 'We call all hangmen Jack Ketch now, and that is because the real Jack Ketch – the chief hangman at that time – was so hated. It was he who executed Monmouth. I was there when he was beheaded. *Butchered* would be a better word.

'Monmouth paid him six guineas and begged him to do a swift job, but to no avail. The first time he dropped the axe he hit the block and only nicked Monmouth. It took four more blows of the axe and a sharp knife to finish the job. Ketch was lucky to leave the scaffold alive, the crowd were so sickened by what they had seen.

'But no less shameful were the hundreds of hangings that took place throughout the West Country. So many men were killed. It was a shameful thing, Tom; a shameful thing. Let's hope that history is not about to repeat itself.'

'But what happened to Thornley?'

'Well, he managed to escape. He's a remarkable

man. Then, when James was deposed, he was recruited as a government agent.'

'And you married Mary?'

'Neither her parents nor mine wanted us to wed, but they could see that we were in love and had the goodness to put their prejudices to one side. Her parents had moved from Scotland to try and give their children a wider outlook on life, away from the provincial politics of their homeland. But Jamie always had a romantic attachment to Scotland's past. The Act of Union nine years ago was a great blow to him; to see the Scottish nation joined to England and swallowed up in this new nation of Britain. And then to see the Stuarts sidelined in favour of a German prince.'

'And what of Mr Thornley?' asked Tom.

'Daniel was devastated when Mary chose me,' Dr Harker told him. 'Though his pride would not allow him to show it. He attended the wedding. He wished us well. But it was plain to see that some part of him had died. He had taken to his new profession with the same zeal with which he had followed Monmouth. I have barely seen him since, until that day on Tower Hill.'

'How did your wife die, sir?' said Tom. 'If you don't mind me asking.'

'She was murdered, Tom.'

'Murdered?' said Tom. 'Why?'

'That's just it,' said Dr Harker. 'For no reason at all. She was the victim of street robbery and fought back. She was a proud woman and wasn't going to give up her purse without a struggle. She shouted for a constable and one of the thieves stabbed her.'

'I'm so sorry, sir,' said Tom.

'Thank you, Tom,' said Dr Harker. 'I do not talk about it and I try hard never to think of it.'

'That's why you were so keen to help,' Tom realized. 'When Will was murdered. Even though he was a thief himself.'

'Yes, Tom, I think it is. She meant the world to me. I was away on my travels when it happened and it was weeks before I even got the news. I missed the funeral, of course, and Mary's parents have never spoken to me since. I think they blame me for her death because I was not here to protect her. But not Jamie – he knew how Mary encouraged me in my work.'

'But what did Jamie want when he visited you?' said Tom.

'He came to give me this.' Dr Harker took a locket on a gold chain from his pocket and, after opening it, passed it to Tom.

'This is your wife, Dr Harker?' asked Tom, looking at the tiny painting.

'Yes, Tom,' said Dr Harker. 'That's my Mary.'

'She was very beautiful.'

'She was. She certainly was. Jamie risked his life to

bring that to me. Do you see why I have to help him, Tom?'

'Yes, Doctor,' said Tom. 'I do.'

'Jamie is in Newgate now. Daniel has bribed a turnkey to set him free and I am to furnish him with sufficient funds to leave the country and join his comrades.' Tom nodded. 'You realize that to give money to a known Jacobite would be a hanging offence at best,' said Dr Harker gravely.

'At best?' said Tom with a wry smile.

Dr Harker did not return it. 'At worst it might mean being drawn and quartered too. To have your innards ripped out while you're still alive, Tom. To be hacked up, boiled and spiked on Temple Bar.'

'So you refused?'

'No,' replied Dr Harker. 'Refusing Jamie would be like refusing Mary. I agreed to get him his money if it meant he might be safe. Everything is in place. I deliver it tomorrow.'

'Will you . . . ?' began Tom. 'Will you be all right, sir?'

Dr Harker smiled. 'I don't know, Tom,' he said. 'I hope so.'

Tom had never seen the doctor look so worried or try so hard to seem as if he were not.

'Now, Tom,' Dr Harker went on, 'I have to leave you for an hour or so. The Royal Society is holding a lunch for a visiting German scholar, and we are all keen to prove ourselves the more intelligent.' Tom smiled. 'Could you go through the contents of the small chest and get them ready for when I return?'

'Of course, sir,' said Tom. 'And thank you for confiding in me.'

Just as he was about to leave, Dr Harker turned back to Tom. 'Are you really thinking about going with Mr Greaves, Tom?' he asked.

'Yes . . . That is . . . I don't know,' mumbled Tom. 'I think I ought to at least think about it. I do want to see something of the world, sir. For myself, I mean.'

Dr Harker patted Tom on the shoulder and said farewell, leaving him alone in the study.

Tom heard the front door slam as Dr Harker left, went over to the wooden chest the doctor had indicated and opened the lid. A wonderful smell emerged, as if some exotic, tropical air were being released from its captivity. And inside the box there was a piece of cloth made up of thin, multi-coloured stripes. Tom lifted it to find a polished wooden figure of a black man, beautifully carved. He held it up and looked into its eyes.

Suddenly he was aware of a movement to his left. At first he thought he had imagined it because the room was so clearly empty, but no; the movement was outside the window. He crept over to see a man shinning down the drainpipe. He bolted out of the study, running down the stairs two at a time, out of the front door and down the steps and skidding round the corner, headlong into a person standing at the foot of the wall.

'Watch out, Tom!' he shouted. It was Nathaniel Greaves.

Tom stood staring at him. 'What were you doing? Were you trying to break into Dr Harker's study?' he shouted.

'What?' said Greaves indignantly. 'Have you lost your mind?'

'I saw you with my own eyes!'

'You did, did you?' said Greaves.

'Yes, I did,' said Tom. 'You said you'd changed.'

'Do you really think I was thieving?'

'Well, why else would you be up a drainpipe?' said Tom.

'I wasn't up no drainpipe, you goose!'

'Well, I don't see anybody else here!' Tom waved his arms, pointing around them.

'He wasn't likely to stick around, was he?' shouted Greaves. 'In any case, you cheeky sprat, I wasn't no burglar, I was a— Well, no matter – I wasn't no burglar.'

'I know what I saw,' said Tom.

'No you don't,' said Greaves. 'You know what you *think* you saw. It *wasn't* me! And I ain't standing here to listen to my own flesh and blood sing false witness, neither! You watch yourself, Tom. A man like that won't think twice about killing if he's cornered. You're in danger, Tom. Mark my words.'

'A man like what?' shouted Tom, but he shouted to an empty courtyard. Greaves had gone.

## 11

# The White Rider

Dr Harker mounted his horse, patting him on the neck and smoothing down his mane. The horse snorted and shifted its weight, scraping a horseshoe across the cobbles. The doctor brought out the locket and opened it. He looked at Mary's face, sighed, closed it again and returned it to his pocket. Thornley, who was still recuperating at Dr Harker's house, stroked the horse's face and looked up at his friend.

'She would have been proud of you, Josiah,' said Thornley. 'You take care, do you hear? It doesn't feel

98

right staying here and watching you go like this.'

'You have done enough, Daniel,' said Dr Harker. 'Wait here and . . . well, I shall see you when I return.'

'I shall be here. Everything will be fine, Josiah,' Thornley reassured him. 'I know it will.'

Dr Harker was about to set off when Tom came running into the courtyard. 'Good day, Mr Thornley. Dr Harker!' he gasped. 'I thought I might have missed you. I'm coming with you!'

'No, Tom,' said the doctor. 'I thank you – sincerely. But I cannot ask this of you.'

'You don't have to ask,' said Tom. 'I've made my mind up, sir. I'm coming with you. I'm your assistant, am I not?' Dr Harker smiled.

'You're a brave lad, Tom,' said Thornley, and he too smiled one of his customary broad smiles. 'Josiah has told me that he has confided in you. I'm sorry if I gave the impression that I did not trust you. My business is all about secrecy.'

'I understand,' said Tom. 'It's forgotten.'

'Splendid!'

'Very well, Tom,' said Dr Harker. 'To tell the truth I shall be glad of the company.'

The doctor hired a horse for Tom from a nearby stables and the pair set off along Fleet Street, heading west towards the Strand and the setting sun. They turned right and north onto Drury Lane, riding through the clamour of Covent Garden, as the usual throng headed for theatres, coffee houses and clubs, while hawkers and pickpockets did their best to relieve them of their purses.

The crowds began to thin as Tom and Dr Harker reached Tottenham Court Road, and in no time at all they had left the metropolis behind them and rode with open fields on either side, heading towards Hampstead and Highgate as dusk became darkness.

The night was clear and cold and an amber full moon was rising above them. Tom was a city boy through and through, and the featureless blackness all around them was alien and disturbing. An owl shrieked out like a strangled man and he gripped the reins as though his life depended on it. It seemed an age before Dr Harker pointed and said they were approaching their rendezvous point: a gnarled and broken oak that looked like a clutching hand. But there was no sign of McGregor.

To make matters worse, just as they were approaching the tree, Tom could see two riders coming towards them. The strangers stopped their horses and, though they were too far away to hear, Tom could tell by the movement of their heads that they were speaking to one another. After a few moments they kicked their horses on.

'Blast it!' said Dr Harker.

'What shall we do, sir?' asked Tom.

'Have your wits about you,' the doctor replied in a

whisper, staring ahead. 'Most likely they are fellow travellers and as nervous of us as we are of them.' Tom found it difficult to imagine how anyone could be as nervous as he now felt, but he tried hard not to show it. 'Jamie will stay hidden until they are gone, that is for sure.'

Gradually, the two riders came close enough for Tom to make them out a little more clearly. One was a rich-looking gentleman in a periwig and tricorn hat; the other a black man wearing a powdered tie-wig.

'Good evening,' said Dr Harker. 'How do you fare?'

'Well, thank you,' replied the gentleman. 'It is good to see a friendly face on such a lonely road.'

'That it is,' said Dr Harker, taking off his glove and offering his hand. 'May I introduce myself? I am Dr Harker of Fleet Street, London, and this is my assistant, Thomas Marlowe.'

'I am Henry Drayton,' said the gentleman. 'Once of Boston, Massachusetts.' He shook Dr Harker's hand without taking off his glove. Dr Harker put this down to different manners in the Colonies, but as he gripped Drayton's hand, he was struck by something odd about it. Tom felt it too when he in turn shook the hand.

Tom and Dr Harker looked at the black man at Drayton's side. Drayton followed their gaze and raised one eyebrow. 'Oh – this,' he said, as one might speak of a boot or a dog. 'This is my boy, Caliban.'

The 'boy' Caliban was, Tom thought, about twenty-five years old, though it was difficult to tell by moonlight. On mention of his name, Caliban looked up and nodded to Tom and Dr Harker.

'Good evening,' said Tom.

'Good eve—' began Caliban before being cut short by a vicious slap on the side of the head from his master.

Tom was shocked by the suddenness of this violence and his horse jittered, shaking at the bridle and twitching its legs nervously.

Drayton smiled at Dr Harker. 'You would not believe the money I had to pay for this dullard,' he said. 'It is getting harder and harder to buy a decent slave. This creature is worse than no help.' He hit his slave again, and this time it was Caliban's horse that jumped, lurching forward, almost throwing its rider off.

'Stop it!' cried Tom. 'Leave him alone!'

Caliban lost one foot from his stirrup and lurched towards Tom, who grabbed his arm to keep him from falling. Caliban clung to him and struggled back into the saddle.

'I see you have had no experience of slaves, young man,' said Drayton. As Caliban returned to his side, he raised his arm to strike him again, but quick as a flash, Dr Harker moved forward and grabbed his sleeve.

'What is the meaning of this!' he shouted. 'I cannot stop you from beating this man in an hour's time – would that I could – but if you strike him again in my presence, I will have to knock you down, sir!'

Drayton looked for an instant as if he were going to put this to the test, but he could clearly see that Dr Harker was a man of his word and thought better of it. He shrugged him off but lowered his hand to hold the reins.

'In Massachusetts, sir,' he told the doctor, 'this would not be countenanced. There a man is free to treat his slave in any way he likes.'

'You see no irony in the word "free" and the word "slave" appearing in the same sentence, then?' said Dr Harker. 'Have no fear, there are many places in England where you can exercise that freedom. But in this small place, for these few minutes, we will pretend that we are all men and all deserving of respect.'

Drayton snorted in derision and was about to say something when he stopped and squinted over Tom's shoulder. 'What the . . .?'

Tom turned in his saddle and looked behind him down the road they had just travelled. In horror he saw another figure riding towards them – a tall man dressed in black. Under his hat, clearly visible in the moonlight, there was no face but a white skull. It was the White Rider.

Dr Harker and Tom turned their horses to face the

highwayman as he approached.

'Gentlemen, may I have your attention?' he called out in a strange, gruff voice. They all stared dumbstruck. 'Splendid, splendid,' he went on. 'I am the White Rider. I have four pistols and I am a very fine shot. Just give me what I want and none shall be harmed. Resist and all will die.'

Drayton laughed and turned incredulously to Caliban. 'What is this?' he shouted to the highwayman. 'What kind of fool joke is this?' He kicked his horse forward. 'You dare to—?'

The White Rider raised a pistol and shot Drayton as he rode forward.

Drayton fell back, still holding the reins, wheeling the horse round to face Tom, who now saw a fierce white glow burning in his chest, which took hold and sent up a plume of smoke to obscure his head as he finally fell from his horse to lie face down on the ground. The White Rider stared at the fallen Drayton in a kind of trance, but this was broken when the sound of hooves broke the silence.

Tom turned to see Caliban galloping away, back the way he had come. The White Rider drew another pistol from his waist and took aim, but there was little hope of hitting anyone at that distance and he turned back to Tom and Dr Harker.

'Very well, then,' he said. 'Now these interruptions are at an end, gentlemen, can we complete our business and be done, without any more foolishness? I have here a sack. Would you be so kind as to place all your valuables in it?'

The White Rider told Tom to ride forward; Tom turned to Dr Harker, who nodded. Tom urged his horse towards the highwayman. As he got closer, he could see that the skull was painted on over a real face, but his sense of dread did not diminish with that knowledge. He could now see eyes glinting in the black sockets but, demon or not, the highwayman had just killed a man in cold blood with little provocation. Tom took the sack that he was offered and rode back to Dr Harker.

'Quickly, gentlemen, if you please,' said the White Rider. 'And do not try to withhold anything from me. I can take the goods from your corpses if need be.'

Tom could see that Dr Harker knew there was no point in resisting: the doctor reached inside his coat for the bags of coins he had brought for McGregor.

'Splendid, splendid. Well, well,' said the White Rider, as he heard the coins jingling. 'It seems my luck is improving.'

Dr Harker put his watch in the sack and the locket McGregor had brought him with the portrait of Mary. He began to unbuckle his sword, but the White Rider put up his hand.

'No, no. You may keep your sword. These woods are full of rogues. And you, boy,' he said, turning to

Tom. 'What have you for the sack?'

Tom took his purse from his pocket and emptied the few coins it contained into the sack.

'Is that all?' said the White Rider. Tom did not reply. 'I said, is that all?'

'Yes,' said Tom.

The highwayman leaned forward and stared into Tom's eyes for what seemed like an age and then smiled. 'Splendid,' he said. 'Very well, then. Bring me the sack.'

Tom did as he was told and returned as quickly as possible to Dr Harker's side.

'The White Rider bids you adieu, gentlemen,' said the highwaymen. 'Go back to London.'

'But we have business here,' said Dr Harker.

'Not any more.'

'And what about this man?' said Dr Harker, pointing at Drayton's body. 'Are we to just leave him here like a dog?'

'Well,' said the White Rider, 'you have a choice. You can either leave him or join him.'

Dr Harker stared at the White Rider for a few seconds. 'Come on, Tom,' he said, urging his horse on.

Tom followed suit. Neither of them looked back.

They rode on in silence for half a mile until Dr Harker suddenly stopped his horse. Tom pulled on his reins and came to a halt beside him. To Tom's surprise, the doctor grabbed hold of the collar of Tom's coat and pulled him across so that his face was only inches away.

'Never do anything like that again, Tom,' said the doctor, angrier than Tom had ever seen him.

'I don't know what—' began Tom.

'Your watch, Tom. You could have got both of us killed for that damned watch.'

'My father gave me that watch!' shouted Tom. 'Mr Marlowe, I mean . . . my uncle!'

'And your uncle could have bought you a new one!' Dr Harker shouted back. 'I'm sure he would rather buy a watch than a coffin! That locket was very special to me too, Tom,' he said, finally letting Tom go and lowering his voice. 'I have so little to remember Mary by. I can never get that back.' He looked into Tom's eyes. 'Yet I gave it up gladly to preserve our lives, Tom. There are not many things worth dying for, lad. A watch is certainly not one of them.'

'I'm sorry, sir,' said Tom. 'I wasn't thinking.'

Dr Harker kicked his horse and moved off. Tom watched him ride away, still dazed by all that had just occurred, until the fear of the dark and the surrounding moors overcame him and he bolted after him.

Thornley was waiting for them when they returned and Dr Harker explained what had happened.

'Of all the accursed luck. And you saw no sign of Jamie?'

'None,' said Dr Harker. 'One can hardly blame him. I think he must have made his escape when the first riders approached.'

'That is a devil of a lot of money to lose,' said Thornley.

'The money does not matter!' Dr Harker pulled off a boot and threw it against the wall. 'It is Jamie who matters.'

'I will have to try and make contact with him.'

'It's too dangerous,' said Dr Harker.

'Let me worry about that,' said Thornley with a smile. 'Danger and I are old friends.'

'I cannot thank you enough for this, Daniel,' said Dr Harker. 'Do you really think you will be able to find him?'

'It is my job, after all,' said Thornley with a smile.

'But where will you start?'

'I don't know. But I will start now.' With that Thornley tipped his hat to them both and headed out of the courtyard.

'But it's the middle of the night!' shouted Dr Harker.

'The night I also count among my very closest friends!' he shouted over his shoulder.

# 12

# A *freshly* DUG GRAVE

'Tom,' said Dr Harker a few days later, 'put down that pen. We have an appointment and we do not want to be late.'

'An appointment?' asked Tom, looking up from his writing. 'Who with?'

'Dr Cornelius,' said Dr Harker, grabbing his cane.

'Dr Cornelius? I don't understand, sir.'

Dr Harker banged his hand down on a pile of books, sending up a cloud of dust. 'I can do nothing more about Jamie. I am forced to leave that to Daniel.

But I am determined to find out more about this White Rider fellow, Tom,' he said. 'It is not simply the money, though heaven knows that is maddening enough given that it leaves poor Jamie without the funds to leave the country. No, Tom, if it were just the money I would mark it down to the crime-ridden age we live in and let go. I have to confess it is the theft of the locket that angers me so. Besides, I cannot sit back and do nothing while Daniel takes all the risks.'

'But what has Dr Cornelius to do with the White Rider?'

'He has the White Rider's victim, Tom,' said Dr Harker. 'The body of the man we saw murdered was sold to Surgeons' Hall. It is as good a place to start as any.'

Though Tom had been forced to revise his view of surgeons since he met Dr Cornelius during the Death and the Arrow murders, he was still not entirely comfortable visiting Surgeons' Hall. Dr Harker had been sent word that the body of Henry Drayton had been picked up by two enterprising farmers and sold to the surgeons.

Dr Cornelius was waiting on the steps, tall and thin and elegantly dressed as usual, leaning on his cane, his eyes half closed. He shook Tom and Dr Harker warmly by the hand and suggested that they all went across the road for a coffee.

'Now then,' said the doctor once they were all seated. 'What can I do for you, my good friends?' His long white fingers drummed on the tabletop. Tom noticed that there were small round stains on the fringe of the lace that was bunched at his throat and realized with a slight shiver that they were splashes of blood.

Dr Cornelius seemed to guess what Tom was looking at. 'My profession still fills you with horror, does it not, Tom? But this is the only way we can improve our knowledge of the human body, don't you agree? Dissection of the dead will help us heal the living.'

'Yes, sir . . . I mean, no, sir . . . I mean . . .'

Dr Cornelius laughed. 'There are few who do not find it odious, Tom,' he said. 'But one day it will be different. Or so I hope. Now what is it? Do you need my help?'

'You have the body of the man shot by the highwayman they call the White Rider,' said Dr Harker.

'*Had*,' corrected Dr Cornelius.

'Had? Has he strolled off then?'

'No,' said Dr Cornelius with a withering smile. 'He was dead, sure enough. No, he was claimed.' He took a sip of coffee.

'Claimed?' said Tom. 'By who?'

'Well, I was not there myself,' said Dr Cornelius. 'A black manservant turned up with a rather large amount of money as a donation to our work in return for the body of his master. My colleague Dr Bennett dealt with it. I am afraid his interest in the contents of the servant's purse overwhelmed all other concerns. I am sorry I cannot be of more help. What interest do you have in this man, if you don't mind me asking?'

'It's complicated, Jonathan,' said Dr Harker, looking warily around. 'To be honest with you, we don't quite know what we're looking at yet. Until we do, it's best we say as little as possible.'

'Understood, Josiah,' said Dr Cornelius.

'Is there anything you can tell us about the body?' asked Dr Harker.

'Well,' said Dr Cornelius, 'I can tell you that he was shot, but I gather you know that already. I can also tell you he had a burn mark on his chest, though it was certainly the shot that killed him. There was a silver flask in his breast pocket and the bullet went clean through it. It seems to me there was some sort of explosive substance contained therein and the shot ignited it.'

'Extraordinary. But what about his hands? Was there something special about his hands?'

Dr Cornelius smiled. 'Yes, there was. He had a crippling burn there. It was old. It could have been an accident, but I feel sure he had been burned on the hand for theft some years ago.'

'That is why he has wearing gloves!' said Dr Harker. 'I knew there was something odd about his hand.'

'Yes,' said Tom. 'I noticed that too!'

'This business gets foggier and foggier, does it not, Tom?'

'It certainly does, sir,' said Tom.

'You seem to know more about this death than you are saying, Josiah,' said Dr Cornelius.

'Well, I have to confess that I am baffled,' said Dr Harker. 'Tom and I heard an account of a White Rider attack in which a man fell lifeless to the ground after being pointed at by this spectral highwayman. The witnesses say he glowed as if on fire before he dropped.'

'But this man was shot,' said Dr Cornelius.

'Yes. There is something strange about that, I grant you.'

'Perhaps the witnesses were mistaken,' suggested Dr Cornelius. 'Perhaps he always shoots them. Were the bodies of the previous victims examined?'

'No,' said Dr Harker. 'They were never found.'

'Never found,' Dr Cornelius repeated. 'Then we have no evidence either way. In any case, I am merely a humble surgeon' – he got to his feet – 'and I must get back to the hall. I have a dissection at two o'clock and the Prince of Wales is coming to watch. Dreadful bore, but there you have it.'

'Thank you for your time, Jonathan,' said Dr Harker. 'Are you sure there is no other help you can give us?'

Dr Cornelius took a last sip of coffee and looked

around. 'Listen,' he said, leaning forward and dropping his voice to a whisper. 'I should not really tell you this, but the body was taken to St Mary's Church. You may find something there.'

'Thank you again, Jonathan,' said Dr Harker.

'Good luck,' said Dr Cornelius.

As Tom and Dr Harker walked through the church-yard gate, the sexton was filling in a newly dug grave. A robin was ducking his beak into the pile of earth beside him and, after several goes, yanked out a long fat worm and flew off to a holly bush to eat it.

'Good afternoon, my man,' said Dr Harker.

'Uh-huh,' said the sexton, heaving another shovel full of clay into the grave.

'Anyone I might know?' Dr Harker nodded at the grave.

'Depends who you know,' said the sexton. 'It's thirsty work, this shovelling. Awful thirsty.'

Dr Harker tossed him a coin and the sexton caught it in mid air.

'Henry Drayton. Friend of yours?'

'Who paid for the coffin?' said Dr Harker.

The sexton wiped his brow. 'Hungry work, too,' he said.

The doctor tossed him another coin. 'Who paid?' he repeated.

'Black boy, he was. Says his master was this Drayton

fellow's great friend, though it's strange to say that the master weren't here in person for the ceremony.' The sexton put one of his filthy hands into his breeches pocket and pulled out a piece of folded paper. 'I'm to get the headstone carved as well. This is what he wants written on it. Read it, if you can.' The sexton passed it to Dr Harker, who read it and passed it to Tom.

' "As you from crimes would pardoned be," ' read Tom. ' "Let your indulgence set me free." '

'What kind of words is those for a Christian grave, I ask you?' said the sexton.

'They are the last lines of *The Tempest*,' said Dr Harker.

'Opera, is it?'

'No, it is certainly *not* an opera,' said Dr Harker crossly. 'Does no one remember William Shakespeare?'

'Anyway,' said the sexton with a shrug, 'he paid his money so I'll make sure it's done. His master's got plenty of money, I'll say that.'

'But I thought Drayton was his master?' said Tom.

The sexton shrugged again.

'And do you know this master's name?' asked Dr Harker.

' 'Fraid not, but the black fellow's in there now' – he gestured towards the church – 'with the vicar, though if you want my opinion they shouldn't let the likes of 'im in a . . .'

Tom and the doctor ignored the sexton's speech and strode off towards the church. Henry Drayton's black slave, Caliban, was just leaving and walked straight into Dr Harker.

'Now then,' said Dr Harker. 'Just the gentleman we've been looking for.'

The slave kicked out at the doctor with all his might and ran, vaulting over a tomb in the graveyard with Tom in pursuit. Caliban was fast. He sprinted towards a wall that seemed too high to climb, but he leaped onto a headstone and then to the wall, clambering over and jumping down. By the time Tom had run round through the churchyard gate, he was gone.

Dr Harker limped up behind him and they stared down the empty street. 'What the blazes is going on, Tom?' asked the doctor.

Tom could think of nothing to say.

'Why would this Caliban fellow show such loyalty to a man who used him so badly? And why is he running from us now? It doesn't make sense, Tom.'

Dr Harker suddenly slapped the hilt of his sword. 'Tom!' he said. 'You were right. I should have trusted you and Ocean from the start. We need someone with his knowledge of London's criminal fraternity. If there is anything to be learned about this White Rider fellow, Ocean's the man to find it.'

## the BROKEN MAST

'Tom!' said Mr Marlowe as his nephew walked into the Lamb and Lion printing house. 'I ... I wasn't expecting to see you.' Mr Marlowe's big hands flexed and relaxed like a nervous schoolboy's.

'I was looking for Ocean,' said Tom.

Mr Marlowe nodded, and wiped his hands on a cloth. 'I see.'

'Are you well?' Tom asked, instantly regretting the coldness of his last remark.

'Me?' said Mr Marlowe. 'I'm fine, Tom. Yes, yes. I'm fine. How about you?'

'I'm fine,' said Tom.

'Good, good. That's . . . good. And how is Dr Harker?'

'He's well,' replied Tom. 'But he has a problem that Ocean may be able to help with.'

'Does he now?' said a voice behind Tom. It was Ocean.

'Ocean!' said Mr Marlowe, relieved at the distraction. 'Tom's here from Dr Harker's. He needs you on some business or other.' Then he muttered that he must get back to work, that pamphlets weren't going to print themselves, and disappeared from the room.

'He's a fine man, your father,' said Ocean.

'He's not my father,' corrected Tom.

'Sorry, Tom,' said Ocean. 'I wasn't thinking.'

'But you're right,' said Tom. 'He is a fine man.'

'I'm not one for getting involved in someone else's problems, Tom, but this is hard for him too, you know,' said Ocean.

Tom nodded. 'I know it,' he said.

Neither of them spoke for a while until Tom broke the silence to change the subject. 'Look, Ocean, I'm here because Dr Harker needs your help.'

'Then he has it, Tom,' said Ocean. 'What's the trouble?'

'I'll tell you what I can as we walk.'

★　★　★

A few days later, Sarah the maid knocked on the door
to Dr Harker's study and showed Ocean in. Tom and
the doctor shook his hand and then sat down, eager
to hear his news.

'I've made some enquiries just like you asked, Dr
Harker,' said Ocean.

'And?'

'Well,' said Ocean. 'The White Rider is a mystery.
No one knows a thing. Not one single thing. It's like
he really was a spectre.'

Tom looked at Dr Harker.

'He is no ghost, Tom,' said the doctor with a smile.
'Of that I am in no doubt. Did you really discover
nothing useful at all?'

Ocean glanced quickly at Tom and then back to Dr
Harker. 'Well, sir,' he said. 'I can't say, right now—'

'Can't say?' said Dr Harker, furrowing his brow.
'What do you mean?'

'I have an informant who knows something, but I
need you to hear it from his own lips,' said Ocean.

'Why? What is it that you won't tell us yourself?'
Then, seeing that Ocean would not be moved, the
doctor sighed. 'Very well,' he said. 'Go and fetch him and
we'll hear what he's got to say. This is urgent, Ocean.'

'I know that, sir,' said Ocean, glancing at Tom
again. 'It's just that he can't come to us. We need to go
to him.'

'I fail to see the problem, Ocean,' said Dr Harker. 'Take us to this informant of yours. Take us now, if you like. The sooner the better.'

'The problem is, sir,' said Ocean. 'This fellow of mine – this informant – he lives in the Wapping Mint. He's a convict, sir, and he won't come out for fear of Hitchin or some other thief-taker arresting him.'

Tom stared wide-eyed at Ocean. The Wapping Mint was the last of London's criminal 'sanctuaries', where thieves and cut-throats lived by their own rules.

'The Wapping Mint,' repeated Dr Harker nervously. 'I see your point, Ocean. But, nevertheless, if we must go there, then we must.'

'Very well, then. This is for you, Tom.' Ocean reached into a bag at his side and tossed him a cudgel. 'We need to go armed, gents. It will look odd if we don't, and in any case we might need some help. If anyone but the doctor and me comes near you, Tom, give them a tap on the hat rack with that. As for you, Doctor, I know you're a demon with that sword, but it's going to mark you out as a gentleman. Pistols would be better, if you have them.'

'I'll find something suitable,' said Dr Harker. He went upstairs and Ocean leaned towards Tom.

'This is dangerous country, Tom,' he said. 'All our lives are dangling now. Don't talk to anyone. Don't look at anyone. Just stick close by me and listen.'

Dr Harker returned and the three men stood in the hallway.

'We all ready then?' said Ocean.

'I think so,' Tom replied.

'Lead on, McDuff,' said Dr Harker.

Ocean stared at him. 'You won't be saying anything like that when we're at the Mint, will you, Doctor?' he asked.

'Well I . . . No, I suppose not.' The doctor looked a little crest-fallen. Tom smiled to himself.

'Thank God for that,' said Ocean.

The three friends took a carriage to the Tower, just as Tom had done with Greaves, but the area seemed very different now as dusk began to fall. Ocean led them down by the river beyond the Tower, where the water seemed to be so filled with ships that Tom felt he could have walked clear across the Thames, jumping from one to the next.

Lanterns were being lit and rowing boats were working their way among the ships, some to the north shore and some to the south. Sailors called out to one another and Tom could hear women giggling, and from a ship nearby he heard a mournful voice singing in a language he did not recognize. Everywhere there was the background rasp of hemp ropes, the rustle of canvas and the slap of the water against hulls.

'There!' said Ocean, pointing ahead of them. 'That's where we're meeting him.'

Tom peered into the gloom and saw a tavern among the jetties and warehouses. A fiddler was playing at the door and a sign saying THE BROKEN MAST hung above his head.

The tavern was clad in weatherboarding that was so rotten and distressed it looked as if it had been ripped from the hull of a sunken ship, and inside it was as dark as the hold of a cargo vessel, small candles dimly twinkling among the fog of pipe smoke. Ocean made straight for a table in the far corner where three men were sitting, huddled in conversation. As they approached, two of the men immediately stood up and walked away without a word.

Ocean beckoned Tom and Dr Harker to sit down. 'This is Smiling Jack,' he explained. 'He's an old friend of mine.'

'Pleased to meet you,' said Tom with more confidence than he felt. 'I'm—'

'I don't need to know your name,' said Smiling Jack. 'Ocean here has vouched for you and that's enough for me.'

Tom could see that it was not the man's cheerfulness that had won him the nickname. He had a scar which ran from the corner of his mouth, sloping upwards for several inches towards his ear. It gave the effect of a permanent smile, totally at odds with the grimness of his actual expression.

'Tell them what you told me,' said Ocean.

'Well,' began Smiling Jack, 'Ocean here tells me he knows of a cove what's been a King's Passenger and I remembered him straightway as a flash cove who got himself clapped up in the whit for working the rattling lay. He was in this very place only the other night. Never forget a face. Should have been scragged too, as it happens, but caught the ferry instead. Last time I saw him he was in his darbies down by the river. I was seeing off a cull of my acquaintance who'd been done for working the kid lay. Died on the journey, poor devil.'

'There,' said Ocean turning to Tom. 'What do you say to *that*?'

'Er . . . What did he say, Ocean?' said Tom.

Ocean and Smiling Jack laughed. 'He's talking about your father,' said Ocean. 'About Greaves.'

'What about him?'

'Weren't you listening?' said Ocean. 'Greaves worked the rattling lay.'

Tom still looked blank.

'He was a highwayman.'

'A highwayman?' said Tom, turning to Dr Harker.

'Might be an idea to keep your voices down, gents,' said Smiling Jack. 'There's many a man here who answers to that description, but few you would want to meet.'

'So you've brought me here to peach on my father!' shouted Tom.

'I'm peaching on no one!' hissed Ocean. 'I knew you'd never believe it coming from me.'

'So what if he was a highwayman?' said Tom. 'It doesn't have to mean anything.'

'No it don't,' agreed Ocean. 'But Dr Harker asked me to ask around, and this is what I found out.'

'Please,' said Smiling Jack nervously. 'Keep your peace—'

'What's going on here, Jack?' said a man behind Dr Harker.

The doctor turned round and inadvertently knocked the man's drink out of his hand. He stood up at once and said loudly, 'My good fellow, I really am most terribly sorry.'

The tavern went suddenly silent and all eyes turned towards Dr Harker.

'Oh no,' said Ocean under his breath.

'What have we here?' shouted a man with an eye patch at a nearby table. 'We seem to have a Justice of the Peace in the establishment!'

'Or maybe it's the Lord Mayor!' shouted another.

Dr Harker took a step towards them.

'What are you doing, Doctor?' hissed Ocean.

'Allow me to introduce myself!' shouted Dr Harker. 'They call me Gentleman Joss Harker.'

'Do they now!' shouted the first man, getting to his feet. 'And how come we ain't never heard of you?'

Four men pulled out pistols, cocked them and aimed them at Dr Harker. At the same time Ocean stood up, drew two pistols himself and pointed them at the man with the eye patch.

'You gonna shoot us all then, Ocean, with two pops?' said the man.

'I ain't aiming at all of you, Tyler,' said Ocean. 'They're your dogs. You whistle and they come to heel. Well, you better whistle fast, 'cause if one of them so much as sneezes, so help me, I'll blast you to fish bait.' The four men held their ground. Ocean held his. 'My fingers are getting twitchy!' he shouted.

'All right,' said Tyler. 'Calm down. We're all friends here. Garret, Rich, Preacher, Fuller – drop your shooters.'

Ocean didn't move.

'I thought you'd gone respectable on us,' said Tyler with a snigger.

Ocean ignored him. 'He's with me!' he shouted, shoving Dr Harker back to his seat. 'Anyone got a problem with that, then let's hear it.'

'We know you, Ocean,' shouted a man at the back. 'There's no cause for trouble!' There was a murmur of approval and Ocean relaxed and let his pistols drop.

'Yeah, but who is this mate of yours, Ocean?' shouted someone close by.

Suddenly Dr Harker was on his feet again. Ocean made a grab for him but it was too late.

'I have only recently arrived from Massachusetts,' said the doctor, 'where I gained some notoriety for working the rattling lay.'

Tom stared at Ocean, who closed his eyes and slowly shook his head.

'I ain't never seen a highwayman go about the town without his pops,' said a man nearby.

'Pops?' said Dr Harker. 'Pistols? Good Lord, no. Dreadful things. They make such an awful din.'

This statement was met by raucous laughter and Tom saw Ocean take up his pistols; his trigger-finger twitched.

'He don't like the din,' said a bearded man nearby. He was tipping his chair back against a wooden post. 'And how exactly would that work then? How do you get the attention of them as who you're going to tax, if you ain't got any cannons? Do you wave your handkerchief at them, then?'

Dr Harker suddenly reached into his coat pocket and hurled something towards the man. It happened too fast for Tom's eyes to follow, but he heard the thud and turned to see the tomahawk he had been admiring in the doctor's study, stuck through the man's hat, pinning it to the wooden post behind him. The room was silent. The man gingerly lowered his head. The hat stayed where it was.

The room erupted into laughter.

'You're all right!' said a huge man standing next to Dr Harker. He patted him on the back so hard he nearly knocked him over.

Tom looked at Ocean, who raised his eyebrows, shrugged and sat back down.

'He don't like the din!' shouted someone in a mock-aristocratic voice, and everyone laughed again.

'Now if you'll excuse me, gentlemen,' said Dr Harker. 'My friend Tom and I have some pressing business to discuss with Smiling Jack and Ocean Carter here.'

'Give the man his hatchet back,' said Tyler to the other man, who had pulled it from the post and was turning it over in his hand.

'Gladly.' The man raised it above his shoulder and hurled it at Dr Harker. Again Tom only saw the flash as it hurtled by, but the man's aim was not as good as the doctor's and when Tom turned he saw that the huge man who had slapped Dr Harker on the back had blood pouring from his ear. The tomahawk was stuck into the post behind him and had taken a piece of his ear with it as it passed by.

'It might be a good time to leave,' said Ocean, and he grabbed Tom and shoved him towards the door. Dr Harker pulled out the tomahawk and the giant bellowed like a bull and charged forward, knocking chairs, tables and customers flying. Tom, Dr Harker and Ocean made it through the door, as bottles and mugs rained down behind them.

'Gentleman Joss?' said Ocean, as they stood panting outside. Dr Harker blushed. Tom laughed. 'You are an amazing man, sir, and that's a fact.'

'I will take that as a compliment,' said Dr Harker.

'I'm surprised you let the man throw the tomahawk at Dr Harker,' said Tom to Ocean, excited now that the fear had gone from his stomach. 'Did you know he would miss?'

'No,' said Ocean. 'I knew the doctor wouldn't have thrown the thing if he didn't have a plan for when it came back.'

'A plan?' said Dr Harker.

'Yeah,' said Ocean. 'I figured you'd . . . I don't know . . . catch it.'

'Catch it?' The doctor chuckled. 'Oh dear me, no. You can't catch a tomahawk in mid air. Quite impossible.'

Ocean stared at him in disbelief. 'Gentleman Joss,' he repeated, shaking his head. He laughed and turned to Tom, but Tom was thinking of other things.

'Tom?' said Dr Harker.

'It's my father, isn't it?' he said. 'Greaves is the White Rider. All that stuff about changing his ways and taking me to America was all lies—'

'We don't know that, Tom. We don't know anything for sure.'

'Come on, Doctor,' said Tom. 'We know he was a
highwayman in the old days. I saw him spying on
your house and the White Rider was disguising his
voice to hide his identity. It has to be him.'

'You saw him spying on my house?' asked Dr
Harker. 'Why did you not say anything?'

'I don't know, Doctor,' said Tom. 'I could not bring
myself to peach on my own father. I hoped there
would be an explanation.'

'And there may yet be,' said Dr Harker.

Tom looked up at the night sky and then back
to his friends. 'This is all my fault! I should never
have told him anything. I should never have trusted
him.'

'Don't get me wrong, Tom,' said Ocean. 'It was me
who found all this out about Greaves, but there's
things that don't make sense here. It don't smell
right to me. There's something we ain't seeing in all
this.'

'I think Ocean is right, Tom,' said Dr Harker. 'We
need to find out more.'

'Why did he have to come back?' said Tom, looking out across the Thames.

Just then, a man suddenly crashed through the
window next to them and lay groaning among
the broken glass. He slowly got to his feet, dusted

himself down and went back inside to rejoin the fight.

'Come on,' said Ocean. 'Let's leave this place, while we still can.'

# 14

# LONDON BRIDGE

Tom was walking home towards Dr Harker's house one evening, stopping occasionally to try and scrape some cow dung from his boot heel, when he looked up to see Nathaniel Greaves standing on the pavement ahead.

'Tom!' shouted Greaves. 'I need to talk to you!'

'Well I don't need to talk to you!' Tom tried to walk past him but Greaves stood in his way. 'I've got ink here for Dr Harker. He's expecting me.'

'This is important, Tom.' Greaves grabbed hold of

his arms. 'You've got to listen!'

'I know you were a highwayman!' shouted Tom.

Greaves stared at him and let go. 'Look, Tom—' he began.

'Don't!' shouted Tom. 'I don't want to hear any more lies!'

'You've got it wrong, Tom. I'm here to see Dr Harker myself.'

'Dr Harker?' said Tom. 'What do you want with Dr Harker?'

Suddenly, over Greaves's shoulder Tom saw someone he recognized skulking beside the courtyard entrance and then moving away down Fleet Street towards the City. It was Caliban.

'I've got to go,' said Tom.

'Tom!' shouted Greaves. 'This can't wait.'

But Tom wasn't listening. He was too intent on not losing sight of Caliban as he moved through the crowd.

As he followed as close behind as he dared, Tom began to notice that Caliban would occasionally stop and skulk in a doorway or flatten himself against a wall or stand on tiptoe, peering down the street. Tom recognized these movements because they mirrored his own. Caliban was following someone. But who? Tom strained to see, but he could not see that far ahead.

The route they took was a meandering one: first

east, then north, then south, but all the while they
were gradually heading down the river towards
London Bridge. The crowds began to thicken as they
neared the bridge. Dozens of hawkers and street
traders lined the pavement to take advantage of the
traffic passing through. An oyster girl with a freckled
face and bright pink fingers winked at Tom and gave
him a dimpled grin. He blushed and hurried on his
way.

Tom struggled to keep Caliban in view as they
started across the bridge – a street of shops, taverns
and houses stretching across the river – but saw him
stop outside a shop and, after a pause to glance
around, go in.

A few seconds later, Tom reached the shop itself. It
was old and dilapidated and was seemingly unoccu-
pied. Over the door, hanging from a rusting tangle of
curlicues, was a cracked and peeling painted wooden
sign showing a golden parrot. Above the bow-fronted
window the sign said: THOS. PARROT, GLOVE-MAKER.

A breeze was picking up and the sign creaked as it
swayed to and fro. It was a melancholy sound, almost
like a groan, and it filled Tom with an unnatural feeling of foreboding. But however sharp his sense of
dread, curiosity was a powerful medicine.

The door creaked as forlornly as the sign, and
would not open properly, forcing Tom to squeeze
through into the pitch blackness of the interior. Panic

surged up inside him as he realized that he had not the faintest idea who or what lurked in that darkness, but as his eyes adjusted to the gloom he could see that the room was empty. There was a faint light at the far end, seeping down a stairwell, and Tom edged his way towards it.

The stairs were bare and missing treads in several places. Woodworm and rot were fighting each other for the treads that remained and Tom took a deep breath every time he took a new step for fear that the whole staircase would collapse.

Slowly and gingerly he reached the first floor. The floorboards here were little better than on the stairs and were cracked and eaten away in places, showing the joists and occasionally glimpses of the floor below. From a room at the end of the hall came a noise; the noise of someone pacing the room.

Tom moved to follow the noise, but no sooner had he done so than an arm was clamped around his neck, a hand covered his mouth and a voice hissed in his ear, 'If you want to live, don't make a sound!' Tom's attacker edged him over to a corner at the top of the stairs and turned him round so that they were face to face.

'You!' said Tom. It was Caliban.

'Be still, if you want to live,' he whispered. Tom could see he held a cocked pistol in his other hand.

'Good advice!' said a voice behind them as a pistol

butt flashed through the air. A second later the slave was lying at Tom's feet and Thornley was standing over him.

'What on earth are you doing, Tom?' he said with his usual broad smile. 'Are you trying to get yourself killed?'

'Thank you, Mr Thornley,' said Tom, rubbing his throat. 'But wait! I heard someone pacing around in that far room.'

Thornley pulled a dagger from inside the collar of his coat. He put his finger to his mouth and indicated that Tom should stay where he was.

Thornley crept noiselessly along the corridor, waited for a moment outside the door that Tom had pointed to and then burst into the room. An ominous silence followed. As Tom was trying to decide what he ought to do next, Thornley called his name.

Tom walked towards the door and found Thornley in the centre of the room.

'Whoever was here has bolted.' Thornley pointed to an open window.

Tom walked over and looked out. Below, the filthy waters of the Thames gurgled through an unseen arch in the bridge.

'It is rather a drop,' said Thornley. 'And this river is a cesspool, but if your life depended on it . . .'

'But who do you think it was?' asked Tom.

'Hard to say.' Thornley had gone back to the landing and was now dragging the unconscious Caliban into the room by his feet. He took some strips of leather from his coat pocket and began tying the slave's wrists and ankles. 'Do you know this fellow?'

'He is the slave of the man killed by the White Rider,' said Tom.

'So he is,' said Thornley, looking at Caliban more intently. 'This just gets stranger and stranger, does it not?'

'He seemed to be following someone,' said Tom.

'And you have no idea who it could have been?' said Thornley.

'No, sir,' said Tom. 'He was too far ahead.'

'And did you tell anyone what you were doing, Tom?'

'No, sir,' said Tom. 'There was no time. I saw Caliban and thought it best to get after him as best I could.'

'Splendid, splendid,' said Thornley with a wide smile.

Something raised the hairs on the back of Tom's neck, but he had no idea what it was. His nerves seemed to be tingling and trying to warn him of something . . . but what? He heard the words, 'Splendid, splendid,' echoing in his ears. Then it came to him.

'*You* are the White Rider!'

# 15

## THE Open WINDOW

'Me?' said Thornley nonchalantly. 'Why, Tom, I think I hear Bedlam calling. I was at Dr Harker's house, remember? How could I have left the house and returned without his nosy maid and cook seeing me?'

'Yes . . . Yes . . . Of course . . . It was *you* I saw, not my father, climbing down the drainpipe!' said Tom. 'It was you! You must have been climbing out of your room . . . You were practising . . . seeing if you could get out of the house unseen.'

'This is all pure fantasy, Tom,' said Thornley. 'And this is the thanks I get for saving your life just now!'

'You were here already – it was *you* in this room!' shouted Tom. 'Of course! You didn't follow *me*; Caliban was following *you*! You recognized him just now, when I said who he was. And how could you have recognized him? You could only have seen him if you were there that night as the White Rider.'

'I'm sorry, Tom,' said Thornley with a grin. 'You understand that I will have to kill you now, don't you?' His pistol lay on the floor between them. He could see Tom looking at it and his grin widened. 'Go on, Tom. Try to get it. Let's add some sport.'

'Leave the boy be!'

Tom and Thornley both turned to the sound of the voice. It was Nathaniel Greaves, holding a sword.

'Well, well,' said Thornley. 'Isn't this touching? The prodigal father come to save his son?'

'I won't take much persuading to run you through,' said Greaves.

'I dare say not,' said Thornley, looking at the pistol on the floor. 'The question is, will you reach me before I reach the pistol and blow your head off?'

'We don't ever need to find that out,' said a voice behind Greaves. 'Because have no doubt that I shall drop you before you take one pace forward.' It was Ocean, holding a pistol, with Dr Harker beside him.

'This is my fight, gentlemen,' said Dr Harker,

drawing his sword and pushing himself past Ocean and Greaves.

'But I don't have a sword, Josiah,' said Thornley. 'They tend to get in the way in my line of work, I find.'

'You are welcome to borrow mine, you rodent,' said Greaves.

Thornley smiled. 'I think not,' he said. 'You may hand me over to the authorities, if you wish. You know that they will take my word over yours. And besides, even if they believed you, I am too good an agent for them to lose. Either way I will take my chances.'

'They'd let a man like you walk free while petty thieves swing from the gallows!' said Ocean bitterly. 'I ought to kill you myself.'

'I realize these things must be difficult to understand for someone of your . . . limited intelligence,' sneered Thornley.

Ocean took aim and looked ready to pull the trigger.

'Ocean,' said Dr Harker. 'No.'

Ocean took a deep breath and lowered his pistol.

'How did you find me?' asked Thornley.

'Mr Greaves saw through you first,' said Dr Harker. 'He saw you climbing out of the house.'

'Yeah,' added Greaves. 'I knew I'd seen you before, and I was right. I'd seen you arguing with Noah

Fletcher down at the Three Crowns. I asked around and found out that you had run up some serious gambling debts and I heard too that your life was going to be forfeit unless you came up with the money in the next few days. They gave you a good hiding to show they meant business, didn't they?'

'But how did you find this place?' asked Thornley.

'You didn't think they were just going to let you walk away without keeping an eye on you?' said Greaves. 'They followed you, you chub. It was expensive, but in the end they told me where you were.'

'And you made the whole thing up about McGregor,' said Ocean. 'Jamie McGregor was in Newgate just like you said – I checked with Reverend Purney – but you never had any intention of getting him out.'

'Why couldn't you just have come to me and asked for the money? Do you think I would not have helped you as I was going to help Jamie?' said Dr Harker.

'I did not want your help, Josiah,' said Thornley. 'I did not want to exchange one debt for another.'

'There is no debt between friends,' said Dr Harker.

Thornley laughed bitterly. 'This is why I didn't come to you, Josiah. Always so gracious and magnanimous. Even when you took Mary from me—'

'I did not "take" Mary,' said Dr Harker. 'Mary chose to be my wife.'

'And now she is dead!'

'You blame me for Mary's death?' exclaimed Dr Harker.

'Of course I do! You left her here to fend for herself and she was murdered!'

'And what kind of life would she have had if she had married you?' shouted the doctor. 'Married to some murderous liar!'

'I am what I am because of you!' replied Thornley. 'If I had married Mary I would have been a different man!'

'How dare you blame Mary for what you've become,' said Dr Harker. 'You enjoy your work, Daniel. That is the truth of it. You like to kill.' Thornley smiled but made no response. 'But what I don't understand is why you didn't arrest McGregor earlier,' said Dr Harker. 'You knew he had contacted me, so you were clearly following him. Why did you let him move about freely?'

Thornley sighed. 'He was going to solve all my problems,' he said with a smile.

'How?'

'So he did not tell you then?' said Thornley.

'Did not tell me what?' asked Dr Harker.

'Jamie was in possession of a very valuable item.'

'Was?'

'He was searched on his entry to Newgate and nothing was found.'

'And what is it?' said Dr Harker. 'This valuable item?'

'Well,' said Thornley, 'these coves are damnably secretive. All I know is that it is priceless, and it must, perforce, be small enough to be easily carried and secreted.'

'Jewels?' suggested Dr Harker.

'My thoughts precisely, Josiah,' said Thornley. 'And not just any jewels. I believe they are jewels given by Queen Elizabeth to Mary Queen of Scots as a bribe to buy her good behaviour. It was a wasted gesture, of course, but these jewels seem to have been squirreled away back to Scotland after Mary's death. I believe that Jamie's family was given the task with looking after them.'

'I never thought you a person so concerned with material things,' said Dr Harker.

'Hah!' snorted Thornley. 'There speaks a wealthy man!'

'You are hardly a pauper, Daniel,' said Dr Harker.

'Ah, but I do so love to gamble, Josiah. I have gambled my money away and with it all my dreams of escaping this foul work and sailing away to foreign waters where none know me and I can be something more than the stinking creature the government has made me.'

'Your enthusiasm for cruelty is your own,' said Dr Harker.

'Perhaps, Josiah,' Thornley replied. 'Perhaps. In any event, had I found the Jacobite treasure then I could have paid my gambling debts and we would all have been spared this unpleasantness. But now I must say farewell.'

Thornley made his move. But instead of making for the pistol or the sword, with one swift movement he pulled a knife from his sleeve, grabbed Tom and put the blade to his ribs. Tom could feel the point straining at the fabric of his coat, as if one slight effort on Thornley's part would cause it to burst through and bite into his flesh.

'Very well then, gentlemen,' said Thornley with a smile. 'I hope you will understand that though I have no desire to harm the young lad here, I will kill him in a heartbeat and without a care or a moment's thought if any one of you takes a step in my direction. Very, very slowly, now; place all your weapons on the floor in front of you. Splendid, splendid. Now kick them towards me.' Ocean's pistol and the two swords skidded across the floorboards. 'Excellent. Now, if you would all be so good as to line up against that wall. That's it. Good. Well away from the door, Mr Carter. Good man.' Thornley edged Tom towards the door and his escape route down the stairs.

'And so I bid you farewell, my friends,' said

Thornley with a little bow, but just as the words left his mouth, the floorboard he stepped on gave way and made him stumble enough for Tom to throw himself free. For an instant there was stillness in the room as Thornley realized that his shield was gone and that the weapons now lay about equidistant between him and Dr Harker, Ocean and Greaves but out of reach of any of them.

He clearly decided that the odds were stacked against him: the doorway was blocked. He tipped his hat, turned and, quick as a snake, made for the other end of the room. Ocean hurled himself to the floor, grabbed his pistol, cocked it and fired, just as Thornley threw himself headlong through the window.

# 16

# CALIBAN

Dr Harker and Ocean ran to the open window in time to see the splash Thornley had made when he hit the water. They waited for him to surface, but nothing appeared save for his black tricorn hat, which bobbed about on the surface like a duck.

'The tide's going out,' Ocean observed. 'Those currents are powerful strong.'

'Maybe so,' said Dr Harker. 'But then so is Daniel.'

'I'm so sorry,' said Tom to his father.

Greaves grinned. 'What for?' he asked.

'For thinking you were trying to steal from Dr Harker,' said Tom, a little embarrassed to even say the words. 'For thinking you were a rogue.'

'Yes,' said Dr Harker, walking over from the window. 'Your father had his suspicions about Thornley right from the start but feared that we would not believe him. He told us that he had tried to warn you about Thornley but you would not listen. We have a lot to thank him for. But what were you doing here, Tom?'

'I followed him,' said Tom, pointing to Caliban, who was just coming to.

'Please, sir,' the slave said with a groan. 'I beg you, sirs. Untie me. Caliban ain't done nobody no harm.'

'I think we'll keep you just like that until we find out what's going on here,' said Dr Harker.

'If it pleases you, sirs, then I will tell you all I know,' said Caliban, flinching as if from an invisible blow. 'If it pleases you, sirs.'

'Speak up then, man,' said Dr Harker. 'But could you do us all the favour of dropping the act? Whatever you are, you are certainly not the cringing fool you are pretending to be.'

After a small pause Caliban returned Dr Harker's smile and then sat more upright. His whole bearing changed in an instant, and Tom noticed how he seemed to have grown to become the biggest man in the room.

'What do you want to know?' he asked.

'Who you are, for a start,' said Dr Harker. 'Who you *really* are.'

'Who I really am . . . Well, that is an interesting question. I am an African, I suppose – though I have forgotten my language and my people . . . even my own name.'

'We thought you might be a little more specific,' said Greaves. 'You're a slave, aren't you? Well, whose?'

'*Was* a slave,' Caliban corrected, giving Greaves a withering look. '*Was* a slave. Now I am a free man.'

Greaves snorted. Caliban stared at him with cool intensity.

'You were born in Africa?' asked Greaves.

'I was. I was taken by men from the north and sold to white men on the coast. Then I was shipped to the Americas.'

'To Maryland or the Caribbean?'

'Maryland. I was not even aware that there were such things in this world as ships and had never seen an ocean. The journey was a waking nightmare, shut up in those stinking holds. I hoped each night that I might die before I woke, and cried each morning when I found that I had survived. Many did not. If we had been cattle they would have taken more care of us.'

Greaves shook his head and walked away to look out of the window.

'And what happened when you got to Maryland?' asked Dr Harker.

'I was sold,' Caliban told him with a cold smile. 'My teeth were checked and my eyes peered into and my body searched for any signs of illness, and I was sold, like a horse. Though not for as much money, naturally.'

'But you are educated.'

'Yes,' replied Caliban. 'My master was rich and learned and it amused him to pass on some of that learning to me, as you might teach a dog to do tricks. To entertain his friends he would ask me to recite poetry or do mathematics. How the ladies laughed and fluttered their fans.

'It was he who named me Caliban, though I had no idea then what the name signified, other than the master thought himself well pleased with the joke.'

Dr Harker saw the puzzled look on the faces around him. 'It is the name of a character in Shakespeare's *The Tempest*,' he explained. 'A creature who is enslaved by the magus, Prospero.'

'Yes,' said Caliban. 'And like Prospero, my master proved himself better than I thought and granted me my freedom on his deathbed. I was free again, though trapped now in a foreign land with no family and no hope of employment; nobody was going to *pay* someone like me.

'I quickly fell to crime and when I was caught by an innkeeper, he said if I would be his slave he would not fetch the sheriff. He chained my legs to stop me from escaping and used me like a dog. I managed to escape and met up with Henry Drayton. We became a team, and a man cannot ever have had a finer friend. We worked our way up the coast to Boston, and then one day Henry slapped the table as we were counting our money and suggested that we should go to England.

'He had been an actor here in his younger days before going to the Americas to seek his fortune, only to be burned in the hand for stealing when the fortune never came. And so we came and plied our trade, surviving by our wits until that fateful night.'

'By your wits?' said Dr Harker. 'What was your trade exactly?'

Caliban smiled. 'We worked the kid lay.'

'The kid lay?' Tom asked.

'They were conmen,' explained Ocean.

Caliban nodded. 'I am near invisible to white people. If they notice me at all, they see a slave; a dullard, something less than the horse they ride. They would not credit me with the intelligence to steal.' He smiled. 'Which made the stealing that much more of a pleasure. I would play the lumbering slave to Henry's gentleman. It worked very well.'

'So that's why Drayton hit you,' said Tom. 'You spoke up when you were supposed to be his slave.'

'Yes,' said Caliban. 'I forgot myself for an instant. Henry was always quick like that. And you, sirs' – he looked at Tom and then at Dr Harker – 'you showed a rare kindness towards me. I thank you for that, ruse or not.'

'I did what any man should have done,' said Dr Harker.

'Hah! *Should*, maybe,' said Caliban. 'But few *would*. You are more rare than you realize. The last man who treated me so well was Henry Drayton. And now he is dead.' Caliban stared ahead as if Drayton was once more dying in front of him.

'I managed to get away in the confusion and returned later to retrieve Henry's body, but when I arrived, a farmer was already loading it into his cart and heading for London. I heard him say that he would sell it to the surgeons and I eventually made my way to Surgeons' Hall and redeemed it. Then, of course, we met again.'

'Why did you run,' said Tom, 'when we met you in St Mary's churchyard?'

'How could I have explained being there? It would have seemed odd, especially after you had witnessed his treatment of me,' said Caliban.

'Seeing you again and hearing of your enquiries about Henry had got me to thinking,' he went on. 'I had sworn revenge on Henry's killer, but of course, I had no idea who he might be then. I needed to try and discover what your interest in Henry really was, and if there was any link between you and the highwayman.'

'Why did you think there might be?' said Dr Harker.

'Well,' said Caliban, 'for one thing, the White Rider was disguising his voice.'

'Yes,' said Dr Harker with a smile. 'We noticed that too.'

'I thought to myself, well, he could be trying to sound more frightening, but if he was disguising his voice along with his face, then he could only be disguising it from you or the lad.'

'Why not from you?' said Tom. 'Could he not have been someone *you* knew?'

'I had never been to England before,' said Caliban. 'And it was years since Henry was here. It didn't seem likely.'

'But how did you find Thornley?' asked Dr Harker.

'Well,' said Caliban, 'I remembered that you told Henry that you lived in Fleet Street – on the night you met us on the Hampstead Road. It didn't take much to find you. I watched the house and noted the comings and goings. I watched and waited for some clue as to who Henry's killer might be.'

'And what did you learn from all your watching and waiting?' said Dr Harker.

'Not much at first,' replied Caliban. 'Everybody seemed to be acting so suspiciously. At first I thought it might be Mr Greaves there—'

'You weren't the only one, by all accounts,' said Greaves.

Tom felt himself blush and Dr Harker coughed nervously. 'And what made you decide it was Thornley?'

'Well, Greaves here and Thornley have similar builds, but it was something I heard Thornley say, even though he had disguised his voice that night—'

'*Splendid!*' said Tom.

Caliban smiled. '*Splendid, splendid,*' he said. 'It was something about the way he said it – I had heard him before when I was watching the house. Then I was sure. Well, almost sure . . .

'I followed Thornley to this lair,' he went on. 'But once here I could not do it. When it came to the doing of it, it took a strength I don't have to pull that trigger.'

'Maybe you ain't the killing kind,' said Ocean. 'No shame in that.'

'No,' added Dr Harker. 'No shame at all.'

'I was just leaving,' Caliban told them, 'when I heard Tom on the stairs. I was sure that if Thornley felt that Tom had uncovered his true nature then he would kill him and I had no wish to see another fellow die at his hands. I tried to warn Tom but it was too late.'

'I thank you for it,' said Tom.

'I thank you too,' added Greaves. 'I almost wish I hadn't sent for Under-marshal Hitchin.'

'The under-marshal?' hissed Caliban. 'You sent for the thief-taker?'

'Calm yourself,' said Greaves. 'He knows nothing about you.'

'He will find a black man with no master,' said Caliban. 'He can do what he likes!'

'I'm sorry. I sent word before I came here. I was sure it was Thornley we were dealing with. I thought we might need some help. He should be here any moment.'

Tom looked at Ocean and then at Dr Harker and he could see the same expression he knew he wore himself. Greaves had done nothing wrong in sending for Hitchin exactly. But the idea of giving anybody up into the charge of that odious man was hard to stomach. Suddenly there was a noise of men coming into the house.

'That'll be Hitchin,' said Greaves and went out onto the landing, with Dr Harker and Tom close behind.

Tom could see the top of Hitchin's hat as he climbed the stairs. The under-marshal grinned as he came up the last flight. 'Dr Harker,' he said. 'Master Marlowe. Mr Carter. We meet again. I'm glad to see that Mr Greaves has a little more sense of duty than—'

There was the sound of a scuffle from the room where they'd left Ocean and Caliban and then a crash. When they went in, Ocean was trying to get to his feet, but slipped back to the floor, holding a hand to his head, blood seeping out between the fingers.

'Ocean!' called Tom, running to help him.

Two of Hitchin's men ran to the window through which Thornley and now Caliban had jumped and looked down at the rippling surface of the river. 'He's gone, Mr Hitchin, sir. Good and gone.'

Hitchin thumped at the doorframe in fury, dis-lodging a sizeable piece of plasterwork from the wall. He stood there for a moment staring intently at the broken window, then his dead-eyed stare moved on to Dr Harker and Tom, who were helping Ocean to sit up, before he turned and led his motley guard out of the building.

# 17

# The LAMB *and* LION

One day in May, Ocean arrived at Newgate with a delivery for the Reverend Purney to find the jail in uproar. There had been a mass breakout of Jacobite prisoners, and though many had been recaptured almost immediately, twelve had escaped, McGregor among them. The reverend loudly regaled The Quill with the story, telling how one particular Scottish giant had knocked him to the floor and would have killed him there and then – had the Almighty not interfered in the shape of a turnkey with an iron bar.

Tom reflected on the news as he looked around the churchyard at St Bride's once again. Bluebells were growing at the base of Will's headstone. There was thunder in the air. It was growing darker, but the green of the grass and of the leaves on the trees was becoming more and more intense. The air was still and heavy and the atmosphere was dreamlike.

The cherub on Will's headstone smiled its crooked smile and Tom heard footsteps approaching behind him. It was his father.

'Tom,' said Greaves. 'I'm not disturbing you, I hope?'

'No,' Tom replied. 'I was just leaving. Goodbye, Will.'

'Dr Harker said I'd find you here,' said his father. 'Will was a friend of yours, I gather.'

'He was,' said Tom as they walked towards the gate. 'Look, I need to say I'm sorry.'

'Sorry? What can you have to be sorry for?'

'Sorry that I thought ill of you.'

Greaves grinned. 'You thought me a rogue, Tom. And who can blame you, for rogue I have certainly been, most of my life.'

'But you really have changed,' said Tom.

'I hope I have,' said Greaves. 'I needed to. And I could do with changing a little more. I have a temper I'm not proud of. But you have a temper yourself, I notice.'

Tom smiled sheepishly.

'The true rogue in all this was that snake, Thornley,' Greaves went on. 'I've met some fearsome men in my time, Tom, but . . .' He shook his head, half in wonder and half in disbelief.

'Yes,' agreed Tom.

'See here, Tom, the plain truth is that I am a very wealthy man,' said Greaves. 'Bellingham left me land when he died. I sold it for a hefty profit and bought a ship. Now I own three. Fortune shined on me and the thing that would finish it off is if you would join me, Tom.'

'I don't know,' said Tom.

'Come on,' said Greaves. 'Come to America with me, Tom. Come and make my business Greaves and Son. Let me try and make amends for all those years I deserted you. I know I can't make it all right, but I can try.'

'I have a life here,' said Tom. 'People here who depend on me.'

'Well, Dr Harker's a fine man. But he ain't your kin, boy. He has a son of his own, I've heard.'

'He does,' said Tom. 'But he relies on me, I know he does. And then there's my fath——' He blushed.

'Mr Marlowe can handle his own affairs,' said Greaves. 'Don't get me wrong, Tom. Old Marlowe has done a fine job with you – a better job than I would have done – but he don't need you like

I do. That Carter fellow seems able enough.'

'I just don't know if I could leave,' said Tom.

'Leave what? Leave this dunghill? Why not, lad? I'm offering you a chance to get away, and don't tell me that you haven't dreamed about it, because I can see it in your eyes whenever foreign lands are talked of. And I ain't suggesting transportation, lad. You can come back, you know.'

Tom smiled. 'I know. It's just . . .'

'Look,' said Greaves. 'It's a big step. A mighty leap. I know that. You hardly know me and what you do know ain't especially flattering. But if you come with me, Tom, I'll show you a different Greaves. And I'll show you the world too. Do you want to spend the rest of your days listening to tales of Dr Harker's adventures or do you want to have some of your own?'

'I'm sorry,' said Tom. 'I still need some time to think things through.'

'I'm sorry too,' said Greaves. 'Time's the one thing I can't give you, Tom. I've stayed in London far too long as it is. I take the coach to Bristol tonight. If the coach don't shed a wheel – or get interrupted by highwaymen – I should be there in a couple of days' time. My ship is waiting and the crew restless to sail. We're bound for Africa for our trade, and then America. Hear them names, Tom: Africa. America. Take the coach with me, and they won't be the stuff of dreams no more. Will you come, Tom? Will you, lad?'

Tom looked up at the sign of the Lamb and Lion as if he had never seen it before in his life. The strange face of the lion, so unlike the real lions he had seen at the Menagerie, seemed full of sadness as it looked down at him. That face, with its huge, limpid, human eyes, had frightened him as a child. The lamb resting in its paws seemed so small and vulnerable. It had never been clear to Tom whether the lion was guarding it or about to eat it. A flash of lightning lit up the sky as he and Dr Harker approached the printing house.

Dr Harker seemed to sense the conflicting emotions swimming around in Tom's mind and gently put his hand on Tom's shoulder.

'You have made the right decision, Tom,' he said.

'I know,' said Tom. 'I know it.' There was a distant rumble of thunder.

Dr Harker took two steps forward, turned the brass handle of the shop door and opened it with a smile. After a moment's hesitation, Tom entered. Ocean appeared in the doorway leading to the printing house, ink smeared across his forehead like a bruise.

'Tom,' he said with a smile. 'Dr Harker. Good to see you both.'

'And you, Ocean,' said Tom. 'Is he in?'

'Out the back, sorting out the yard. Keeping

himself busy, more like. Go on. He'll want to see you.'

Tom left Ocean and the doctor and walked through the printing house to the doorway through to the cobbled yard beyond. He stood and watched his uncle stacking empty barrels and smiled, remembering that he always did this at times of crisis. Then all of a sudden, Mr Marlowe saw Tom standing there and froze. He put down the barrel he was carrying.

'So,' he said. 'How are you, lad?'

'I'm well,' Tom replied. 'Though a little ashamed of myself for the way I spoke to you.'

'It's forgotten, Tom,' said Mr Marlowe. 'You had cause enough. I've wronged you. I know that.' Lightning flashed again and there was a loud burst of thunder above them.

'It's forgotten,' said Tom.

Mr Marlowe smiled. 'Greaves has asked you to go with him, I gather.'

'Yes,' said Tom. 'He has.'

'So. You have the chance to travel at last, like you've always wanted.'

'Yes.'

'And what of Dr Harker?' asked Mr Marlowe, picking up the barrel again.

'I have told him that I need to be with my *real* father,' said Tom.

'Fair enough,' said Mr Marlowe with a sigh. 'You can't—'

'And I told Mr Greaves the same thing,' said Tom.

For a moment Mr Marlowe did not seem to understand what Tom was saying, and he stood there with a puzzled expression on his face, until finally the meaning of Tom's words sank in and a look of un-contained joy flashed across his face like the sun bursting out from behind a dark cloud.

'Tom,' he said, tears welling in his eyes. 'I . . . I . . . don't know what to say.'

'I know, Father,' said Tom. 'I know.' And the two of them hugged as though Tom really had gone away to the Americas and had come back after many years.

'But you must not call me Father, Tom,' said Mr Marlowe, wiping the tears from his eyes. 'I reckon Greaves has earned the right to own that title. And I'm as proud to be your uncle.'

Tom nodded. Rain began to beat steadily against the window panes.

'But what about your travels?' asked Mr Marlowe eventually. 'What about America?'

'America can wait,' said Tom.

# 18

# Another BODY IN THE THAMES

When a body was washed up on the banks of the Thames, Tom and Dr Harker once again made a visit to Surgeons' Hall. Dr Cornelius told them that the body had been in the water some time; too long to identify it. But Dr Harker insisted that he must see it for himself. Tom waited in the hallway and he had never seen his friend look so grim as when he emerged.

'The clothes are certainly Daniel's,' said Dr Harker. He swallowed deeply. 'Much else it is impossible to say.'

Dr Cornelius reached into his pocket and pulled out a watch. He handed it to Dr Harker. 'They found this, Josiah,' he said. 'He was found by an honest man who handed it to the constable – who rather unusually was also honest. Do you recognize it?'

Dr Harker nodded. 'Yes. That is Daniel's watch. His father gave it to him when he left for university. I remember him receiving it. Despite everything I still feel sad.'

'You feel sad for the boy you knew,' said Tom.

Dr Harker smiled. 'Yes, Tom. And maybe for the boy I was.'

Dr Cornelius recognized that sentiment and shook Dr Harker's hand. 'If I can be of any more help, Josiah,' he said, 'you know where I am. I still owe you a thrashing at chess. Goodbye, Tom.'

'Goodbye, Dr Cornelius,' said Tom.

Tom and Dr Harker walked slowly back towards Fleet Street, taking the back lanes and alleyways to avoid the crush of shoppers and hawkers. In an otherwise deserted courtyard two red kites were squabbling over the remains of a discarded pie and took to the air in panic as the pair approached.

'You've made Mr Marlowe a very happy man,' said Dr Harker.

'And Mr Greaves a miserable one,' added Tom.

'Worse things have happened to him,' said Dr Harker. 'He seems to have a flair for falling on his feet.' Tom tried to force a smile. 'Mr Greaves is a slaver, isn't he, Tom?'

Tom stopped and stared at him. 'Yes, he is,' he replied. 'But how did you—?'

'It was a guess,' said Dr Harker. 'He promised to show you Africa and America and he seemed to know something of that business.'

'Yes,' explained Tom sadly. 'At first he spoke only of trade and cargo and I was on the verge of taking him up on his offer. Then, that day when he met me at Will's graveside, he finally told me what his "cargo" was. Then I just couldn't go. I couldn't do it. I don't know why.'

'Because you are a good man, Tom,' said Dr Harker. Tom had never been called a man before and he blushed a little. 'I'm proud to know you. May I shake your hand?'

'Of course, sir,' said Tom. 'Gladly.'

The two friends shook hands and then resumed their walk. Suddenly, they heard a familiar voice behind them:

'Gentlemen! What a pleasant coincidence.'

'Daniel Thornley!' said Dr Harker, grabbing the hilt of his sword. 'But . . . But how? I saw you dead . . . I saw your body!'

'Apparently not,' said Thornley with a grin. 'Come now, it was a simple enough matter to disguise that corpse. I was sad to lose my watch, but it was worth it. I would thank you to keep that sword sheathed, Josiah. I would hate to have to shoot you. But that won't stop me from doing so.'

'Your argument is with me, Daniel,' said Dr Harker. 'Let Tom go.'

'No!' Tom shouted. 'I'll not leave you, sir.'

Thornley laughed. 'Such loyalty you inspire, Josiah,' he said. 'It is as well that I am not sentimental.' The smile disappeared. 'I'm afraid I need more money, Josiah. All of it.'

'I thought your debts were paid.'

'Some, yes,' said Thornley. 'But a man like me runs up many debts, and not all of them can be paid so easily, and not all with money. I have a sudden desire to travel, Josiah, and there are those who want me to stay.'

'And not through friendship, I dare say,' said Dr Harker.

Thornley laughed again. 'Do you know, Josiah, I think you were the very last friend I ever had.'

'And how do you expect me to find money for you at this hour?'

'I am afraid that is *your* problem,' said Thornley, smiling. 'But I dare say that if I put a pistol to this lad's head, it is a problem you will quickly solve.' Thornley's attention was suddenly distracted by a drunk, who came tottering down the steps behind him and slumped in a doorway holding a keg of gin.

He turned back to Tom and Dr Harker, to find the doctor reaching for his sword again.

'Ah-ah-ah, Josiah,' he said, wagging his finger as if talking to a child. 'I'll take that.' He took Dr Harker's sword and threw it over the wall behind them. 'Don't play with me, Josiah, or you will see this lad killed and neither of us wants that.'

'I don't think you care who you kill!' said Dr Harker. 'What a monster you have become!'

The drunk groaned and muttered to himself.

'A monster? Listen to that,' said Thornley. 'I risk my life every day for the likes of that! For scum like that! I ask you, Josiah – is that right?'

Dr Harker did not reply. The drunk began to sing tunelessly to himself.

'I never intended to take money from you, Josiah, but as you know, I had run up debts with men who want them paid, and promptly. Had I found the jewel these Jacobite rogues were carrying, all this would have been avoided. I caught one of the rascals, but try as I might I could not persuade him to tell me where the item was. But I believe you met the man in question. After your visit to the opera.'

Tom realized that Thornley was talking about the Jacobite who was pulled out of the Thames. Thornley had killed him.

'McGregor was arrested before I could get to him and then the idiots at Newgate let him walk out. No doubt he is on the Continent with his friend James Stuart and I am left here with a problem. I am a marked man. These Scots take these things personally, as you know, Josiah. I have already had two attempts on my life. In short, I need to find employment in some foreign land, where my enterprising spirit will be appreciated. Russia perhaps. Those Muscovites appreciate a man with my abilities.'

'You have no sense of loyalty to your friends or to your country!' shouted Dr Harker. Thornley hit him round the side of the head with the pistol and he dropped to the floor.

'Dr Harker!' shouted Tom, coming to his aid. The doctor groaned and held his head.

'Get me the money that I need, Josiah, and I will go. Refuse and I will kill you and the boy.'

While Thornley had been talking, the drunk had risen to his feet and was shuffling towards him. 'Go away,' said Thornley without looking round, but with one deft movement, the drunk had a knife at Thornley's throat.

# 19

# A Lock of Hair

'**D**rop the gun!' he hissed. Thornley hesitated for a second. The knife blade was pushed a little harder into his throat. The gun clattered to the cobbles. The man reached inside Thornley's collar and took out a knife, hurling it away down the alley. 'Turn round and face me.' Thornley turned and his attacker now placed the point of his knife at his chest.

'James McGregor,' said Thornley, smiling once more. 'I should have known. Those idiots in Newgate couldn't keep a dead cat caged for more than an hour.

# A Lock of Hair

Why they don't just shoot you people on sight, I will never know.'

'Be still!' said McGregor. 'With your left hand, and using your thumb and little finger, I want you to take out the knife you keep in your sleeve and then the one in your waistband.' Thornley smiled and did as he was asked.

'You killed Malcolm, you coward,' McGregor went on. 'He was scarcely older than the lad standing there. Killed him because he would not tell you about the treasure you sought to steal. What kind of man are you? You believe in nothing. You are hollow.'

'And what kind of man are you?' shouted Thornley. 'Maintaining friendship with the man who let your sister die in the street!'

McGregor threw Thornley's knives across the alley. 'I would rather Mary died knowing the few happy years she had with Josiah, than think of her with an animal like you.' He ripped a button off his coat and thrust it towards Thornley. 'Well, man? There it is, take it!'

Thornley laughed a dry laugh. 'What foolery is this? Kill me and be done with it.'

'Take it!' shouted McGregor, and Thornley picked up the button. 'You'll find the back will come away, if you prise with your fingers.'

Suddenly Thornley looked interested. He turned the button over and hurriedly fiddled with it until, sure enough, the back of the button flipped open like a locket. Thornley grinned and grabbed at the contents.

'But what is this?' he said suddenly. 'Is this some sort of joke? Does this pass for wit in the highlands?' He studied the contents of the button with an expression somewhere between bafflement and fury.

'It is no joke,' said McGregor. 'That is the treasure you have killed for. And treasure it is, too, and priceless. It is a lock of hair from a queen. The one you call Mary Queen of Scots.'

There was a look of utter disbelief on Thornley's face that lasted several seconds, before he raised his eyes to the night sky and began to laugh. It was a wild and humourless laughter and it ended only when McGregor leaned forward and shouted in his face.

'I'll tell you why Mary did not choose you, Daniel.' McGregor used Thornley's Christian name for the first time.

Thornley composed himself and his face became an expressionless mask. 'And why is that?' he asked.

'Because she was frightened of you! Aye, frightened of you! She saw you for the devil you are!'

Thornley suddenly lunged forward, yelling 'No!' at the top of his voice, grabbing McGregor's arm and forcing it up in the air, so that the knife now pointed to the sky, clamping his other hand round McGregor's throat. The force of the attack took the two men clear across the alley and McGregor slammed into the wall at the other side.

Thornley banged McGregor's hand repeatedly against the wall until he was forced to drop the knife. With his free hand, McGregor punched Thornley in the ribs and Thornley let go of his throat long enough for him to make a lunge for the knife.

As McGregor leaned forward to retrieve the knife, Thornley kicked him hard in the face and he collapsed semi-conscious on the cobbles. Thornley adjusted his coat and dusted himself down. McGregor tried to raise himself from the ground, but as he did so, Thornley kicked him again and McGregor rolled over onto his back.

'Stop!' shouted Tom.

Thornley looked round. Tom had picked up the pistol and was holding it in both hands, pointing it at Thornley, who smiled and kicked McGregor once more.

'Stop!' shouted Tom again. 'I will shoot! I will!'

Thornley turned to face him again and smiled at him as one might have smiled at a bothersome child. 'You will find that there is a lot more to pulling a trigger than moving your finger,' he said. 'You're a clever lad, Tom, but have you got the steel to look in my face and send me to the grave?'

Tom took aim again, but the pistol had begun to

feel heavy in his hands and he found it a struggle to stop them from shaking.

'Well, have you, Tom?' Thornley had begun to walk towards him, knife in hand. 'But maybe you're worried that you'll miss? Have you ever fired a pistol before, Tom? I don't suppose you have. And you've only one shot, of course. You don't want to waste it, do you? I'll make it easy for you. I'll come a little closer – how about that? Splendid, splen—'

McGregor leaped on Thornley from behind and knocked him to the ground. The two men rolled over and over across the cobbles, first one way and then the other, with neither appearing to gain the upper hand, until suddenly they came to a halt and for a moment lay motionless on the ground.

Then Thornley slowly got to his feet. Tom looked at McGregor and saw his white shirt dark and wet with blood. McGregor looked at the blood and put his hand to his stomach, searching for the wound. Thornley looked down at him and grinned; then he pulled a knife from his own chest and dropped lifeless to the ground.

'Put the pistol down, Tom,' said Dr Harker gently. He had finally come round and was sitting up. Tom stood in a kind of trance. 'Tom,' repeated the doctor. 'Put the pistol down.'

Tom watched McGregor get to his feet and walk over to look at Thornley's body, and came to his

senses. He looked at the pistol in his hands and then
at Dr Harker getting unsteadily to his feet. He let his
hands drop and his friend put a hand on his shoulder.

They walked over to Thornley's body. McGregor
was searching through his pockets.

'Here, Josiah,' he said, handing him the locket with
the portrait of Mary. 'Keep better care of it this time.'

Dr Harker smiled fleetingly, but then stared down
grimly at the body of Daniel Thornley. 'I cannot help
feeling in some way responsible . . .' he began.

'No, Josiah,' said McGregor. 'You have nothing to
reproach yourself with. Daniel Thornley was evil.
Maybe he always was but we were children and could
not see it. In any event, the man you loved died long
ago.' Dr Harker nodded. 'We must away, Josiah,' urged
McGregor. 'We cannot be found with his body.'

'I cannot just leave him here,' said Dr Harker. 'Like
a dog in the gutter.'

'You will be hanged, Josiah, if you are connected
with his death.'

'And what of you, Jamie?' said Dr Harker. 'How
will you get to the Continent? I can get you some
money if you give me a couple of days.'

'Thank you, no, Josiah,' said McGregor. 'France
has had its fill of us, I think. No, I'm going home.'

'But what of James Stuart and your comrades in
exile?'

'James Stuart!' McGregor closed his eyes as if in

pain. 'Och, he was in Scotland for forty-five days, Josiah! Forty-five days! He'll not come back. Brave men were willing to lay down their lives for him – *did* lay down their lives and *will* lay down their lives – but I'll not fight for him again. I would give my life gladly for my country, but I will not waste it. There'll be another time. Scotland is not done yet. Besides, my father has been ill and my mother needs me.'

'I'm sorry to hear that, Jamie,' said Dr Harker. 'I always liked your father. Though he never had much time for me, I seem to remember.'

'He liked you well enough, Josiah,' said McGregor with a smile. 'He was just too stubborn to show it. Stubbornness is a McGregor trait, as you may know.'

Dr Harker smiled and nodded. 'Goodbye, James,' he said, holding out his hand.

McGregor shook it and nodded to Tom. He turned and started to walk away. Something fluttered along the ground and came to rest on Tom's shoe. He bent down and picked it up. It was the lock of hair that Jamie McGregor had carried in his button. Tom ran after him, and he turned at the sound of the approaching footsteps. Tom held out the lock of hair and McGregor took it, squeezing it in his fist as if trying to gain strength from it. He managed to say a whispered thank you before turning and walking away once more.

'He still has to make it to Scotland,' said Tom as he walked back to Dr Harker.

'I think he will manage,' said the doctor. 'Now, Tom, I want you to fetch Dr Cornelius. Whatever Jamie says, I cannot leave Daniel here like this. We are not far from Jonathan's house. Do you remember the way?'

'Yes, sir,' said Tom. 'But what about you?'

'I'll be fine, Tom,' said Dr Harker. 'I will hide the body behind those steps and wait for you to return. Quickly now.'

Twenty minutes later, Dr Cornelius arrived driving a small cart, with Tom sitting next to him. They lifted Thornley's body into it and covered it with blankets.

'I cannot thank you enough,' said Dr Harker.

'Nonsense,' said Dr Cornelius. 'I shall take the body to Surgeons' Hall, Josiah. I suggest you and Tom get home before anything else happens. I will speak to you tomorrow.' He flicked the reins and the cart trundled off.

Dr Harker clapped Tom on the back. 'Come, Tom,' he said. 'We'd best be off as Dr Cornelius says.'

'Do you think that lock of hair really is from the head of Mary Queen of Scots, sir?' said Tom as they started to walk towards Fleet Street.

'Well, Tom,' said Dr Harker. 'When the Queen of Scots was executed, the axeman held up her head, just as we saw at Tower Hill, only to discover the hair that covered it was a wig. So' – he smiled – 'it may be a lock of the wig of Mary Queen of Scots.'

Tom shook his head at the idea that men might have died for the false hair of a long-dead queen.

'But you see, it does not matter, Tom,' said Dr Harker, 'Whether it was the hair from her head, the hair from her wig or the hair from a wolfhound. It is what men believe it to be that matters.'

# 20

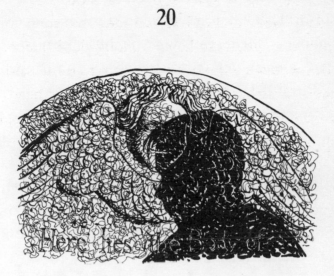

# *The* Tempest

'Well, Will,' said Tom with a sigh, as he visited his friend's grave again. 'Here I am, a Londoner still. Maybe my father's offer of travel will be the last I get and I'll stay here all my days.' He sighed at the thought and looked across the graveyard to the rooftops and spires of the City, with the dome of St Paul's rising above them. 'Still,' he said, turning back to the carved cherub on Will's headstone, 'there are adventures enough to be had in this town, it seems.

'You're about the only one I can talk to about the things that have happened over the last weeks, Will,' said Tom. 'Dr Harker has forbidden me and Ocean to talk about it, for fear of what might happen to us all if anyone found out. It's as though it never happened, Will. But it did.

'Jamie McGregor managed to get back to his family, though not without difficulties. He worked his passage on a Newcastle-bound collier. In Newcastle he was about to board a ship to Edinburgh when he saw government men on the quayside and was forced to travel overland as best he could, sleeping out on the moors and sheltering in barns and outhouses.

'He must have told his parents about how Dr Harker had risked his own life trying to help him, because a few days ago the doctor received a letter from them saying they were sorry for the way they'd treated him and wished for a happier time in which the doctor "and his young assistant" might visit them in Scotland.' Tom smiled. 'I know it's not America, but it's better than nothing!' He chuckled to himself.

'And as for Thornley,' Tom went on. 'The day after he was killed, me and Dr Harker went to Surgeons' Hall. Dr Harker wanted to give him a decent burial but Dr Cornelius said it was too dangerous; that if someone found out whose body it was we would all be done for.

'Dr Harker agreed and Dr Cornelius said he

should leave it to him. He would deal with the body.'
Tom shuddered and screwed up his face. 'It's best not
to think of how old Cornelius will "deal" with the
body, eh, Will?' And Tom tried, unsuccessfully, to put
the subject out of his head. 'Still,' he added, 'it's no
more than Thornley deserves, if you ask me.'

Dr Cornelius's caution was well founded. The public
mood towards the Jacobites was still one of paranoia
and hostility, and a few days later more Jacobites met
their ends in London, drawn through the streets on
hurdles. They were dragged behind horses, all along
the cobbled streets, to Tyburn's Triple Tree, there to
meet the most terrible of all deaths: the traitor's death.
Crowds jeered from balconies and windows and
spat and cheered from pavements while children
laughed and frolicked behind the soldiers as if it were
a parade. At Tyburn the men were hanged and taken
down while still breathing to be hacked about and
butchered with less mercy than the pigs at Smithfield
to chants of 'God Save the King!'

That same night Tom and Dr Harker were at the
theatre again, this time with Ocean for company. It
had been Dr Harker's idea that they should go and see
a performance of *The Tempest*, Shakespeare's story of
the wizard Prospero and his daughter Miranda, of his
spirit servant Ariel and his monstrous servant Caliban.

Tom was captivated by the magic of the play,

though he found it hard to keep up with what was
going on. Ocean nodded off very near the start and
began to snore, despite frequent nudges from Dr
Harker. The actor playing the character Caliban wore
a costume covered in scales and feathers and rags. He
shambled about the stage and could not have seemed
more different to the quick-witted other Caliban.
Even so, Tom found himself sympathizing with this
monster, who now found himself ruled over by
Prospero in a land that had once been his by
right.

When Prospero's daughter said, 'O wonder! How
many goodly creatures are there here! How beauteous
mankind is! O brave new world/ That has such
people in't!' she was talking about the men who were
shipwrecked on the island during the tempest, but
Tom found himself thinking of all the people who
had made the things he and Dr Harker were
cataloguing. He found himself thinking of the events
of the last weeks. He thought about Jamie McGregor
and he thought about Thornley. He thought about his
father, Nathaniel Greaves, and the grim cargo he
carried. And he thought about Caliban the African,
as Prospero was addressing the audience for the
last time:

> 'And my ending is despair,
> Unless I be relieved by prayer;

The Tempest

Which pierces so, that it assaults
Mercy itself, and frees all faults.
As you from crimes would pardoned be,
Let your indulgence set me free.'

Later that evening, the three friends stood outside the
front door of Dr Harker's house. It was still warm and
the sky looked like blue satin. Bats were hunting
moths, swooping around the lantern over the door.
No one seemed to want to instigate the parting.
Ocean broke the spell finally by bidding Tom and the
doctor good night and turning to leave.

As he did so, the sound of hooves grew like a clap
of thunder, and into the courtyard came a horse and
rider. Ocean reached for his pistol but Dr Harker
grabbed his arm. The rider pulled his horse to
a skidding halt on the cobbles and lifted his
head. Tom looked on in horror. It was the White
Rider!

The highwayman pulled on the reins and the horse
reared up on its back legs and then clomped down
again onto the cobbles. The White Rider lifted his hat
and, holding it to his chest, made a slow bow to them,
then he replaced his hat, turned and cantered out into
the street and away.

'What's going on?' said Tom. 'How can that be?
Thornley's dead. We saw him killed.'

'Are you sure, Tom?' asked Ocean. 'It wasn't

another trick? These people are slippery as eels.'

'No,' said Dr Harker. 'I have been so stupid, Tom. Thornley *is* dead. There is no doubt about that. Do you not see what this means?' He turned to face Tom and Ocean. 'It's obvious! There were *two* White Riders!'

'Two?' exclaimed Tom. 'But how?'

'Thornley only *pretended* to be the White Rider to steal from me. He could hardly have been expected to do all those other robberies. That was the real White Rider.'

'But then who the devil's the real one?' asked Ocean.

'Caliban!'

'Caliban?' said Tom and Ocean simultaneously.

'Do you not see?' said Dr Harker. 'Daniel Thornley's plan to dress as the White Rider and rob us would have worked perfectly had he not chanced upon the *real* White Rider that night. Henry Drayton and Caliban were a team, just as Caliban said, although I think that it was Caliban, rather than Drayton, who was the brains in the company.

'Drayton played the part of the victim in the robberies. They worked the kid lay, just as Caliban told us. They fooled the travellers in the stagecoaches into believing that the highwayman had supernatural powers. Drayton fired a blank charge at Caliban. Caliban pointed his finger, and while Drayton's back was turned to his audience he set off a flash, making it seem as if he had been hit by some invisible force. He then dropped the charge and fell, apparently lifeless, to the ground. The terrified passengers would now be very co-operative. Once robbed, the coach drove off and Drayton could come back to life ready for their next adventure. It really is delightfully conceived.'

'Drayton had the charge in his pocket,' said Tom. 'That's why there was the explosion when Thornley shot him.'

'Yes,' said Dr Harker. 'That must have come as rather a shock to Daniel.'

'But can you really be sure of this, sir?' asked Ocean.

'Not of everything, of course,' said Dr Harker. 'But I am reasonably confident of my conclusions.'

'Well I'll be . . .' Ocean shook his head, turned away and chuckled to himself.

Dr Harker suddenly clapped his hands together. 'Of course!' he exclaimed. 'How stupid of me.'

'What is it, sir?' said Tom.

' "As you from crimes would pardoned be, Let your indulgence set me free," ' said Dr Harker.

'Dr Harker?'

'You let him go, didn't you?' said the doctor, turning to Ocean.

'Let him go? Let who go? What do you mean?'

'Caliban. I would have thought it plain enough,' said Dr Harker, laughing.

'Maybe you missed that bump on my head, Doctor,' said Ocean. 'But it was there sure enough.'

'I think you told him to hit you, Ocean,' said Dr Harker. 'After you'd untied him, of course. He hit you hard enough to leave a bruise but not to do you harm. You feigned the rest.'

'And why would I do a thing like that?' asked Ocean. 'Aiding a man like that. Why, that's a hanging offence in itself. Why would I do that for a slave? For a man I never met?'

'Because you did not want to see him hang,' said Dr Harker slowly. 'I know that sentiment myself, remember. You did not know he was the White Rider then, but you still had good reason to believe that as a black slave convicted of thievery, hanging would be his fate. For what it's worth, Ocean, I would not have seen him hang myself, White Rider or not.'

'Nor I,' added Tom.

'So we need speak no more about it, then, as we are all agreed that he was a man worth the saving,' said Dr Harker. 'Ocean's intervention will be our little secret.'

'Agreed,' said Tom.

'You certainly have an colourful imagination, Doctor,' said Ocean. 'It would make a good ending for one of your books.'

'Indeed it would,' said Dr Harker with a smile, clapping both Tom and Ocean on the back. 'Indeed it would.'

## About the Author

Chris Priestley was born in Hull in 1958, spent his childhood in Wales and Gibraltar, and his teens in Newcastle-upon-Tyne. He has been a successful illustrator for many years, working mainly for newspapers and magazines. The first book he wrote, *Dog Magic!*, was published in 2000 and shortlisted for the Children's Book Award. Since then he has written several books for children, both fiction and non-fiction. He lives in Norfolk with his wife and son.